I0654065

THE SONG OF THE THRUSH

A Tales of the Latter Kingdoms Novel

CHRISTINE POPE

Dark Valentine Press

THE SONG OF THE THRUSH

ISBN: 978-1-946435-09-5

Copyright © 2017 by Christine Pope

Published by Dark Valentine Press

Cover design by Ravven

CHAPTER 1

"LORD SORTHANNIC SEDASSA, DUKE OF MARRIC'S Rest," my father's steward intoned, and I sat up a little straighter in my chair. The duke had been something near to a recluse ever since he was spurned by the Crown Princess of our kingdom nearly two years ago. True, Princess Lyarris had broken her engagement with the duke in order to marry the Hierarch of Keshiaar, the ruler of that vast desert empire, and so one could not precisely say that Lord Sorthannic's jilting was of the common sort. Even so, rather than accept his rejection as the matter of state that it most certainly was, the duke had retreated to his estate of Marric's Rest and never returned to court. He left his town house in Iselfex shuttered and dark, and turned his back on the society of others. To add fuel to the gossip about his hermit-like existence, it seemed that he had also taken on something of the appearance of a wild man, his hair long and unkempt, a thick beard now obscuring what I had heard had once been quite handsome features.

That the Duke of Marric's Rest might journey here to my father's estate of Silverhold to bring his suit surprised me greatly. For one thing, it was passing strange that such an exalted being as a duke would come to pay court to the daughter of a mere baron, even if her father happened to be one of the richest men in the kingdom. Our holdings took their name from the extensive silver mines located in the hills a few miles to the east of the castle where I had grown to adulthood, and so our wealth far outstripped the fairly humble title to which my father had been born. The size of my dowry made me quite the matrimonial prize, but so far I had not met a single man who stirred my heart, or who convinced me that his hand in marriage would be a suitable exchange for the freedom I currently enjoyed.

Both of my brothers' marriages had been arranged nearly from birth, and during the seven years between the time my next-oldest brother Evander was born and my mother finally bore me, my parents lost three daughters. Indeed, my own arrival in this world was so harrowing that my mother did not survive more than a fortnight after my birth. During those two weeks, however, she begged my father to allow me the freedom to choose the husband of my heart, rather than be forced into a union that might end in sadness. While my parents' marriage, though arranged, had been a happy one, her own sister had suffered at the hands of the man her parents had chosen for her, and died young. So my father, who loved my mother dearly, agreed despite his misgivings, for he wanted to make sure that she passed into the next world untroubled by her daughter's fate.

So I grew to adulthood unhindered by any unwanted betrothals, and when I reached my eighteenth year, those men who wished to become my husband—and share in the wealth I would bring to the marriage—began to come to Silverhold to plead their cases. I describe their endeavors in that way because truly, it did seem more that they were making pleas to the crown for a boon, rather than expressing their admiration of my person, as one might expect of a man who wished to make his suit to a young woman he found desirable. My lady's maid, Sendra, had always exclaimed over my beauty, and the mirrors hung about the castle reassured me that she was not lying merely to puff up the vanity of the baron's only daughter. Still, it seemed that the size of my dowry far outshone any delicacy of my features, for such qualities seemed to be mentioned only as an afterthought, and not as my primary attraction.

My father must have noted the way I sat up in my chair and sharpened my attention upon hearing Lord Sorthannic's name, for he murmured to me in an undertone, "Be on your best behavior, Marenna. It is true that his Grace has behaved somewhat oddly the past few years, but he is still one of the greatest peers of this realm. Do not let your tongue run away with you."

"I have no intention of allowing it do so," I replied with some asperity. Truly, I was rather nettled that my father would think so little of my manners. Yes, there were some who probably thought that I had been allowed to run rather wild, and that I did little to guard my speech, but I saw nothing wrong with being honest, as long as such honesty was taken at face value and not used as a weapon to cause others hurt. Besides, it was not my fault that those who had come before Lord Sorthannic should be such sorry specimens. Perhaps if my mother had known what a meager selection I would have to choose from, she might have decided it was better for me to have an arranged marriage after all. Judging by those peers I had met at balls and dinner parties at my brothers' homes, or at the family town house in the capital, it seemed that all those who would have made a respectable husband had already been snatched up.

My assurances did not seem to have mollified my father overmuch, for he still wore a faint frown, his dark eyes worried underneath his greying brows. However, he fixed a smile on his face and stood, gazing down the center of the hall, where the Duke of Marric's Rest was about to make his entrance.

I also rose from my chair, and disposed my skirts of heavy claret-colored silk so they might fall in graceful lines. This was one of my most becoming gowns, one that enhanced my dark hair and eyes and pale skin, and I hoped it would catch the duke's eye. For surely he must have quite discriminating taste, to have been betrothed to the Crown Princess, who was a very great beauty. Clearly, no other ladies had captured his heart since her.

How could they? I asked myself. *It is very difficult to lose one's heart to a stranger if one's life is ordered in such a way to avoid all society.*

But then the duke entered the hall...

...and I felt my heart sink, for it appeared the rumors about his appearance had been true. Surely this must be a wild man from the hills, rather than one of the kingdom's greatest peers. True, he was finely dressed, in a doublet of black velvet slashed with silver-grey, and a heavy chain of silver and garnets resting on his broad shoulders. But his hair was a dark unruly mass that fell past his shoulders and partway down his back, and the lower half of his face was obscured by a beard so thick and black and pointed, I could not tell what he looked like at all.

Some sound of disappointment must have escaped my throat, for my father drew himself up and shot me a warning glance out of the corner of his eye. I barely registered his disapproval, however, for my mind was already running ahead of itself, wondering what on earth it would be like to attempt to kiss someone with such a beard, to feel that rough, brambly tangle pressing against my lips. No, I had never kissed anyone—my father made sure that I was never given the opportunity, that I was kept as sheltered as possible. His efforts were perhaps unnecessary, for I had never met anyone I even wished to kiss. But I realized that such intimacies were expected between a husband and wife, and so to even contemplate performing such an act with someone as wild and unkempt as Sorthannic Sedassa—

"My lord," he said, bowing to my father.

"Well met, your Grace," my father replied. "I trust you did not have too difficult a journey?"

"Not at all," Lord Sorthannic said. He did have a pleasant voice, warm and deep, with just the faintest trace of a lilt at the edges of some of his words. I recalled then that he had actually been born in South Eredor, more than a thousand miles from his estate of Marric's Rest, and had come here to Sirlende to claim his lands and title as a boy in his teens, not so very much younger than I was now. His gaze flickered toward me, and I saw then that his eyes were an unusual dark blue, the color of the sky just as dusk fell. One rarely saw blue eyes in Sirlende, but I guessed he must have been lucky enough to inherit them from his South Eredorian mother.

Because of the heavy beard that concealed half his face, it was very difficult to guess as to what he might be thinking. Did my appearance please him? Or did he find me as unappealing as I found him?

Somehow I found that difficult to believe. At least I did not look as if I had spent the past two years roaming wild in the woods, subsisting on nuts and berries, with nary a mirror to tell me how unkempt I was, nor a hairbrush to remedy the situation.

"Your Grace, this is my daughter, Marenna," my father said, turning slightly toward me.

I knew what I must do. Although I had not spent much time at court, my lady's maid had taken ample time to instruct me in all the niceties of proper behavior. Assuming a practiced smile, I extended a hand. "I am very pleased to meet you, your Grace."

Lord Sorthannic took a few steps toward the dais where I stood, then lightly pressed his fingers against mine. Yes, his touch was sure and strong, those fingers showing evidence of calluses, which meant he was not the sort of nobleman to sit idly back and leave the management of his estates to others. While the roughness of his hands matched the coarseness of his appearance, I found I was rather pleased to learn that he was not the kind of foppish courtier I'd learned to despise.

But then he bent to lay a kiss against the back of my hand, as custom required. I could not help but flinch, for his beard was so very rough, and felt more as though someone had just brushed a bundle of twigs over my skin.

"Goodness!" I exclaimed, the word escaping my lips despite my promises to my father that I would be on my best behavior. "His beard is as rough as a thrush's nest!"

A grim silence followed that unseemly remark. As soon as I had made my ill-considered utterance, I wished I could take it back, but I was no sorceress, not someone who could stop the hands of a clock and turn them backward. There were not so many people in the hall, for my father was not one who kept a large retinue, but there was still Elsen, our steward, my maid, Sendra, and various men-at-arms to witness my unwitting rudeness.

At once I clapped my hand to my mouth, even as Lord Sorthannic straightened, those dark blue eyes of his seeming to pierce through to my very soul...and find it wanting. When he spoke, his voice was measured, cold. "I am sorry that you find my person so repellent, my lady."

"I—"

He did not allow me to get any further than that single syllable, for he turned toward my father and said, "My lord, I will waste no more of your time. It is clear that your daughter and I will not suit. Have a very good day."

"Your Grace—"

But it seemed that my father's entreaties would have no more effect than mine. The duke presented his back to us, and stalked through the hall and out the tall doors of iron-studded wood at the other end. They had been left open to let in the warm wind of a mild afternoon in late Sevendre, and so he could not slam them shut behind him. However, his displeasure was obvious enough to everyone who was there to witness it.

"Foolish child!" my father snapped, rounding on me as soon as Lord Sorthannic was gone. "I told you to guard your tongue!"

"I am sorry, Father," I said, not bothering to hide the misery in my tone. No, I had felt no attraction to the duke—except to admire those fine blue eyes of his—but he had already suffered enough heartache without me insulting him in the presence of my father's men. Our steward Elsen might be the soul of discretion, but I could not say the same thing for our men-at-arms. No doubt the story would be all over the countryside by nightfall.

"'Sorry'?" my father repeated, clearly not mollified at all. Indeed, in that moment, I hardly recognized my handsome, good-tempered father; his face was red with fury, and sparks fairly flew from his dark eyes. "You have insulted a peer of the realm. You have brought disgrace to this house. Go to your room—I have no wish to look on you any longer."

Flayed by such harsh words, I could only gather up my skirts and flee the chamber, tears beginning to run down my cheeks. I went to the staircase located on the right side of the great entry hall, the one that led up to my tower bedroom on the east side of the castle.

Normally, I enjoyed the time I spent in my rooms, for they offered a splendid prospect of the fields immediately surrounding the keep, as well as a glimpse of the tall, craggy hills where my family's wealth was brought forth from the earth. Now, though, I could only fling myself on my bed and cry stormily, cursing myself for my impulsive nature, for the unguarded speech that had made me insult such an exalted man. Sirlende was a very great empire, but even so, it possessed only ten duchies in all. And I had just disparaged the man who held one of those great titles.

A soft knock came at the door. "My lady?"

"Go away," I said, knowing that my response was just as rude as the words I had spoken to Lord Sorthannic. But I was in no mood to talk to Sendra, who no doubt would scold me—gently, true, but scold nonetheless—for my behavior. Perhaps I deserved such a scolding, and yet, as a young woman of almost twenty, I thought I was far too old to be subjected to that kind of treatment.

However, I also knew that she most likely would wait outside my door until I relented, for she had no duties within the household other than to look after me. I had already acted enough like a spoiled child; it would not do for me to continue exhibiting that sort of behavior.

So I pushed myself off the bed and went to the door and unlatched it, then went back to my bed so I could lie down on it once more. In the process, I was also wrinkling my silken gown, but that hardly mattered now. The audience had come and gone, and I had acquitted myself very badly.

Sendra came in and shut the door behind her. To my surprise, she did not look so much angry as worried, as if she had feared what she might find when she came to visit me.

"I told him I was sorry," I said, knowing that she had come here as an agent of my father, who could not bear to look upon me in his ire. "I do not know what else he expects me to do!"

If she had been my mother, perhaps she would have come and sat down on the bed next to me. However, a servant—even one who had been part of the household for so many years—could not take that kind of liberty. Instead, she retrieved the chair from the little writing table by the window and placed it by the bed, then sat down before reaching out and patting me on the hand.

"I am not sure it is that he expects anything," she replied, her kind, dark eyes watching me carefully. I realized then how much grey had overtaken her hair, and felt vaguely ashamed that I had not noticed such a detail up until now. "This is not the sort of matter that can be easily fixed."

Her words only served to drive home how badly I had behaved. She was right, of course. This sort of insult could not be smoothed over with a few flattering words. Perhaps if my family had been the equal of Lord Sorthannic's, then the situation might not be so dire. However, all our wealth could not quite compensate for the difference in station between the Duke of Marric's Rest and my father, a mere baron. Tears began to gather in my eyes once more, and I reached up to wipe them away.

"Oh, don't weep, my lady," Sendra said. "I am not sure it is quite as bad as that. Your father is in general a most even-tempered man, and not one to hold a grudge."

"I am not so sure about that," I returned. "Yes, most of the time he is quite mild, which makes his anger all the more impressive when it is aroused. I doubt he will forgive me anytime soon.

And the terrible thing is, I truly did not mean to insult Lord Sorthannic. It is only that he looked so very wild, and I had never experienced anything like that scratchy beard of his scraping against my skin. The sensation was most unpleasant."

"I'm sure it was," my maid said. However, while her words made it sound as though she was in agreement with me, something about her expression seemed to indicate the opposite.

"You think I should have held my tongue."

At once she shook her head. "My lady, it is not my place to tell you what you should or should not have done. That is your father's place, and none other, since your lady mother is no longer with us."

No, she was not. I wondered then what it would have been like to have a mother raise me, rather than my father and my lady's maid. My brothers, Randel and Evander, had had something more of her, since Evander was seven when she passed away, and Randel nearly ten. They could remember how she looked, the sound of her voice. But I, who had been an infant only a fortnight old, recalled nothing of her. The only reason I knew what she looked like at all was because of the fine portrait of her that hung in my father's chambers. Truly, she had been very lovely, with her tip-tilted dark eyes and lustrous dark hair. My father always said I resembled her, and if the portrait was at all accurate, then yes, I could see that.

Was it because I looked so much like his late wife that he was doubly disappointed in me, that I had in some way failed his memory of her as well?

I could not bear to think such a thing, but I had to allow myself to believe it might be true.

Tears pricked at my eyes again and I swallowed, forcing them back as best I could. How dreadful that I had blurted out such a terrible insult to Lord Sorthannic! Why could I not have accepted the ritual kiss and kept my thoughts to myself? Perhaps, if I had behaved like less of a child, I could have seen past that bird's nest of a beard, allowed myself to look for the man beneath. And who knows? If I had acted in a more seemly fashion, had eventually become the duke's wife, in time I might have been able to persuade him to shave off the beard, so I might gaze upon his features unobscured by that bushy growth.

Too late for all that, of course. Now I could only hope that the incident would pass without too many dire consequences, and I might gain my father's favor again. He was angry now, but I was his only daughter. Surely he must find some mercy for me in his heart.

However, he sent one of the footmen to inform me that I should eat my supper in my chambers. I did not argue, for what had been phrased like a request was really a command. To tell the truth, I preferred to hide myself away, to give myself some time apart from the rest of the household. My father did not put on many airs, unless we had visitors, and so we generally took our evening meal with the men-at-arms who guarded the keep. At the moment, I did not think I could bear their curious stares.

I did not sleep well that night—an apt punishment for my behavior, I thought. And although I had no real interest in what I wore, the following day I allowed Sendra to dress me in my favorite dark blue gown, the one with the green embroidery around the neck and sleeves. Somewhere in the back of my mind, I thought that perhaps if I appeared subdued and modest and like a good, dutiful daughter, my father would find it in his heart to forgive me. Surely he could not stay angry with me forever.

Since I received no further instructions about remaining in my room, I deemed it safe enough to go downstairs. The light was fine this morning, so I thought it best to go to the solar and take up my embroidery. Again, this notion was born of the idea that doing so would make me look like a well-behaved and biddable child, and not the young woman who had brought such shame on the family the day before. Besides, I did enjoy needlework, for it gave me a chance to show that I was accomplished at something.

It was in the solar that my father found me; it appeared that he had been riding, for he wore his high boots, and a faint scent of leather and horse sweat accompanied him. I did not know whether this was a good sign or not, for while my father enjoyed riding very much, especially during such pleasant, mild weather as we'd been enjoying lately, he also tended to rise early and ride if his thoughts were troubled and he needed time to sort through them.

Unfortunately, I had a feeling that his reasons for riding this morning had everything to do with the latter, and not because he wanted to spend some time in the sunshine.

Still, I made myself pretend as best I could that everything was well between us, and raised my head from my embroidery and smiled as he entered the solar. That smile faltered as soon as I caught a glimpse of his stormy expression, but I knew that to allow my smile to disappear entirely would look even worse.

"Good morning, Father," I said, and secured my needle in the heavy linen so I need not worry about dropping it while we spoke.

"Marenna," he replied.

Oh, dear. Was he so angry that he could not even wish me a good morning, even if such words were nothing more than an empty pleasantry? Still, I did not know how I should proceed, having never experienced such treatment from him before. I had to do something to break the heavy silence which fell between us, though, for with every second that passed, it seemed to grow more awkward.

"I thought perhaps I could send the Duke of Marric's Rest a letter of apology, by way of smoothing things over," I ventured. This was a notion that had occurred to me during the depths of the restless night I had just passed. Whether or not it would do any good, I couldn't be certain, but surely there was at least a small chance that Lord Sorthannic would soften slightly when he realized my unguarded comments hadn't been malicious in nature.

"You will do no such thing," my father replied. "For to send such a letter will only be pouring more salt on his wounds. No, best to let it lie, and hope that he forgets sooner rather than later. If he is finally searching for a wife after all this time, we can only hope that he will be otherwise occupied."

"But—"

"No." The word was flat, and brooked no further argument. I stared up at my father, searching his face for some indication that he would not carry this grudge forever, but I saw none. His lips were pressed together and his gaze cool as he looked down at me, as though I was a stranger and not the daughter he had raised for the past nineteen years. "In fact, I spent this past night thinking about what you did, and how you behaved. I was following your late mother's wishes when I allowed you to make your own choice of husband, but I think that game has gone on for far too long. It is clear to me that you have no desire to select a man to be your spouse, no matter how worthy he might be. For you to reject a duke of the realm—"

"Who looked like he might be one of the *corraghar,* the wild men who roam the hills of North Eredor," I broke in, unable to contain myself any longer. "Surely I am allowed some discretion in my choice?"

If possible, my father's lips thinned even further. "No, I think not. My patience is spent, Marenna. I have let it be known that the first man to pass through the doors of this castle who is not already a member of the household may have your hand in marriage. Perhaps seeing the hand of the gods at work in such a thing will teach you a little humility."

Aghast, I leapt up from my chair. "Father, you cannot mean that!"

"I do," he said, his expression hard. "You had your chance—you have had multiple chances—and yet you spent them all foolishly, believing yourself to be above such things. I am not sure of your reasoning, save that perhaps you either thought yourself better than all those who came to pay you court, or you had no wish for marriage at all, and preferred a life of leisure spent under my roof. Either way, you will find yourself sorely out of luck." He paused there, his gaze flickering about the solar, with its hangings of silk and the warm light that poured in through the mullioned windows. "Enjoy this luxury while you may, for there is a very good chance that it will not last much longer."

Having delivered this pronouncement, he turned and exited the room, leaving me to stare after him in dismay. Worry churned within me. How could he have decided upon such a cruel thing? Was this all just a terrible jest? No, unless I did not know my father at all, he had meant every word he said. And I somehow knew this was not a matter that could be solved by such stratagems as teasing cajolery, or a pleasing smile, as I had used in the past to get myself out of trouble with him. He was angry, angrier than I had ever seen him before.

All I could do now was await my doom.

CHAPTER 2

To my infinite relief, no strangers arrived at the castle that morning. My father had informed me that word had been sent around the countryside as to his peculiar commandment, but either he had done so merely to frighten me, or no one in the vicinity was terribly eager to be my husband. This notion upset me almost more than the thought of being married off to a complete stranger, for—once they had gotten done waxing rhapsodic about Silverhold and the extensive mines that had made my dowry so enticing—most of those who had sued for my hand in the past had certainly been effusive enough in their compliments, praising my beauty, or my grace in the ballroom, or the delicacy of my embroidery, something I had always been rather proud of. Had they all been telling me only what I wanted to hear?

Seeking some reassurance, I went to the mirror in my room and analyzed every detail of my features, from the arch of my eyebrows to the curve of my lips. I did not observe anything there that I had not seen a thousand times before, but now I could not help but wonder if the sum total of all those individual details was somewhat less than I had been led to think. Surely there could be no other reason why there had not been many suitors arriving today, all wishing to claim me in accordance with my father's offer.

But then....

I was in my chambers, pretending to read a book but in actuality replaying that terrible scene of the afternoon before and trying to think of how I might have salvaged the situation, when a knock came at the door. At once my heart leapt into my throat, even though I made myself calmly set down the book and go to answer that knock. Outside was my maid Sendra, her expression grave.

"Your father requests your presence in the hall," she said.

This summons made my stomach churn even more, for I guessed precisely why he had sent for me. How could I walk calmly downstairs and see the gods only knew what horror waited for me? Perhaps this man would be old or fat, or the lowest of the low—a swineherd, stinking of his charges?

No, surely my father must have his limits. Even if he had hardened his heart against me, I could not allow myself to believe that he would marry me off to a swineherd, or someone three times my age. He had only meant to frighten me into better behavior.

That was what I told myself as I followed Sendra down the stairs. To be sure, my legs shook beneath me, but the heavy skirt of my silken gown did well enough to conceal my trembling. I held my head high, for I did not want to betray any weakness. If my father wished to give me a good scare, so be it. I would not allow him the satisfaction of seeing how much he had upset me.

When I entered the great hall where my father received visitors, I saw him at once, standing at the bottom of the small dais that held his great carved audience chair. Next to him was a tall man with dark hair, neatly bound into a long tail at the base of his neck. Seeing the stranger, I felt myself relax somewhat. True, his clothes were simple enough—a shirt of home-spun linen with the sleeves rolled to his elbows, a vest of stained brown suede, breeches of brown wool that had been patched more than once. But even though his back was to me and I could not see his face, I was able to tell that he was tall and well built, with broad shoulders and long, strong legs. If my father truly intended to marry me off to a complete stranger, then better one who was not old and fat.

As I approached, the stranger turned toward me slightly. Ah, gods, he was handsome, with a fine chin lightly dusted with dark stubble, and straight black brows over long-lashed dark eyes. Something about him seemed vaguely familiar, although I couldn't see how that was possible. I was fairly certain I would have remembered someone with such a striking countenance, even if he did happen to be a commoner.

"Master Blackstone, this is the Lady Marenna, my only daughter. Marenna, this is Master Corin Blackstone. He came to the estate looking for work, for his specialty lies in vine-yards and the harvesting of grapes. I told him our land was not suited for that type of farming, and he should head south and east. But I also told him of my wish to see you married."

I swallowed and glanced over at Master Blackstone. His expression was entirely neutral; I could not tell at all whether he found my person pleasing, or whether he was attempting to keep his face blank because he feared any kind of reaction at all might evoke an angry reaction from my father, so obviously his superior.

Apparently not discomfited at all by the other man's silence, my father went on, "He was startled at first, but then agreed...perhaps because I sweetened the pot by offering him fifty gold crowns to take you off my hands."

At that comment, my eyes widened—not with awe at my father's generosity, but rather shock that he should sell me off so cheaply. True, it was a sum that a man such as Master Blackstone probably did not see in a six-month, but it was also a paltry amount compared to the dowry which should have been mine. I opened my mouth to protest, to say I was worth far more than that...and then shut it again. If this stranger was a man of such mean worth that fifty gold crowns seemed like a huge sum to him, then the last thing I wanted was to dangle my dowry in front of him. Besides, while that money should have gone with me upon my marriage, its disbursement lay entirely in my father's hands. If he chose to withhold it, there was not a great deal I could do, save journey to Iselfex and throw myself upon the Emperor's mercy. The odds of my doing so were not very high, since of course I did not have the means to make such a trip...not with my father holding the purse strings that trapped all of my money.

"Indeed?" I said, not bothering to keep the disdain from my voice. "It is good to know that a baron's only daughter can be had so cheaply."

My words seemed to amuse Master Blackstone, for he smiled—showing a set of very strong white teeth—and said, "Oh, that is only insurance against your future usefulness. You have very soft hands, my lady. May I assume that you have never worked in the fields?"

"Of course not," I retorted, indignant that he would even ask me such a thing. A lady of my station certainly would not lower herself in such a way. The extent of my own agricultural pursuits involved cutting such roses from the garden that I found pleasing, and not much else. "We have laborers for that sort of thing."

"Aye, and I am one of them, although it seems that there is no work for me here. We will have to journey hence in search of better prospects."

Although Master Blackstone still smiled as he spoke, I sensed that he was attempting to bait me, to make me protest this ridiculous match and say I would have nothing of it. However, my father had proved so cold and capricious over the last twenty-four hours, I knew I must not assert my independence for fear of facing even worse consequences. Although they had not been used for many years, we still had dungeons below the castle, even if these days they were used to store spare furniture and not much else. But what if I angered my father so much that he had me confined to one of those abandoned cells? Faced by that prospect, I thought that perhaps marriage to this commoner was a better fate. At least he was young and handsome.

"I suppose so," I said haughtily.

"You must go and pack your things," my father said then. "Not too many, of course, for you will have to carry everything yourself. Your maid can help you with the packing. By the time you are done, the priest should be here to perform the ceremony."

Those words, so casually spoken, struck cold fear into my heart. Up until that moment, I could have almost pretended this was a game, a torment devised by my father to teach me a lesson about my prideful behavior. But if he had already summoned a priest, then I knew this was no joke at all.

Did I dare argue? Judging by the glitter in my father's dark eyes, I guessed that would be the very worst thing I could do. Better to be a meek daughter, and do as I was told. Even though I was to be married off to this commoner, perhaps at some point my father would relent, would allow me back into his life. Marriage to a complete stranger seemed far more bearable if I could have my dowry back. We could purchase a modest estate somewhere, perhaps a place where Master Blackstone could grow his vines. My father had said that was this man's field of knowledge, after all.

"Yes, Father," I said, then made a quick curtsey before turning to leave the hall. The whole time, Sendra had been waiting near the foot of the stairs, and now she followed me up the steps to my room, her face pale and stricken.

"I cannot believe your father would do such a thing to you!" she exclaimed once we were safely inside my bedchamber and I had shut the door. "It is too cruel!"

Privately, I was inclined to agree, and yet I knew that it would be better for me to remain silent on the subject than to utter the bitter truth of my angry heart. Instead, I shrugged, then said, "It is what he has decreed, and so I will not go against him."

Her dark eyes narrowed as she gave me a piercing look. "It is not at all like you to be so meek, my lady."

"In this matter, I have not much choice but to be meek."

She still surveyed me, as though attempting to see into my soul and discover the true reason behind my odd behavior. "Well, Master Blackstone is quite handsome—"

Yes, he was. And thank all the gods for that. I did not know precisely what being married to someone entailed, although I believed that kissing was involved, and that at some later date, a baby might come along. I frowned then. Being the youngest of my family, and with my two brothers and their own families settled far enough away that they did not visit very often, I did not have much experience with infants, or small children. Ah, well. There was not very much I could do about the matter now.

"And so I could have done much worse." I went over to the wardrobe and opened the doors, then stared blankly inside. To be honest, I had no idea what on earth I should bring with me. My gowns were all made of silk and velvet, with embroidered trim accented in gold and silver thread, and pearls on a few of the finer dresses. Certainly there was not much I owned that seemed suitable for the rough life which loomed ahead of me.

Apparently sensing my distress, Sendra

hurried over to my side and began to briskly sort through the choices. "This green silk is plain enough, and you have your two linen gowns. You have only used them on the warmest summer days, but they will do to see you through most of the autumn. Perhaps you can ask your new husband"—she seemed to choke on the word, but forced herself to go on—"to get you some material so you might fashion a woolen gown for the winter."

As to that, I had no idea. To be honest, the thought of having to construct a new dress all on my own rather horrified me. My needle might have been talented enough when it came to embroidering a pillowcase or a velvet band to trim a gown, but of course I had never made an entire garment by myself. That had been Sendra's responsibility—or, when an especially fine gown was needed for a particular holiday or a wedding, we sent for a dressmaker from Iselfex. I told myself that it was now only early Sevendre, and the truly cold days would not arrive until late Novendre, so I had some time to puzzle out how to do such a thing.

In the meantime, I had far more pressing matters to worry about, not the least of which was the prospect of being married to Corin Blackstone within the hour.

"Pack whatever you think is best," I told Sendra, and went away from the wardrobe so I might lower myself to the window seat. That shaky sensation had returned to my knees, and I needed a moment to regain my composure.

Sendra gave me a sympathetic nod, and then got out the smaller of my two valises and began laying folded dresses and chemises and pantalets and stockings in it. Once the valise was full and she had buckled it closed, I realized there were still an alarming number of gowns hanging in the wardrobe. I had room to take three or four with me, and no more than that.

"I will take good care of them, my lady," she said, perhaps seeing my sadness over having to leave so many lovely possessions behind. "That is, if I am allowed to."

Her comment made me frown. "What do you mean, if you are allowed to?"

She gave a slight lift of her shoulders, but I could see the worry in her eyes. "It is only that I am your lady's maid, Lady Marenna. If you are sent away from here, off to a life that has no room in it for servants, then where does that leave me?"

Oh, no. I could not bear that. It was one thing for me to suffer the consequences of my rash behavior, but quite another for poor Sendra to be punished as well. She had nothing to do with the foolish words I had uttered to Lord Sorthannic the day before. "I will make sure that my father keeps you on," I said stoutly.

This bold claim only earned me a sad smile. "That is very good of you, my lady, but in truth, if you are gone, there will not be much for me to do here. About the best I can hope for is that your father finds it in his heart to send me to one of your brothers' households—Lord Evander's newest is something of a handful, or so I've heard, and so perhaps I can be of some help."

Yes, my youngest niece was just beginning to walk, and causing something of a terror in the household, according to the lively letters my brother sent me. I had not seen little Janessa since she was a babe in arms last Midwinter, but I could see why Evander and his wife might wish for more assistance. That seemed to be the best solution for my poor maid, and yet the thought of Sendra leaving the estate struck me to the heart. She had been here at Silverhold ever since I was born and had always seemed to me as much a fixture of the place as the grand arch of stone that led into my father's audience hall, or the expensive glass windows that let such light into the building.

Still, better that she go to my brother than be thrown out onto the street, an all-too-common fate for servants who had outlived their perceived usefulness.

Father would never do such a thing, I told myself, and yet I was not sure I could believe that inner reassurance. After all, he was doing nearly the same thing to me, was he not?

"That seems a very good idea," I said, willing my voice to sound calm. I did not want Sendra to see how upset I was.

She knew me too well for that, however. Although she offered only a smile, she came to me and laid a comforting hand on my shoulder, and set the packed valise down by my feet. A few strokes of the brush through my hair, and then she said, "Come, my lady. With your father in such a mood, it is probably best not to keep him waiting too long."

I nodded, and swallowed the dread that seemed to choke my throat. Sendra bent and picked up the valise, then went to the door and held it open for me. Soon enough I would have to carry my luggage myself—for somehow I had the feeling that Master Blackstone would not deign to perform such a task for his wife. Then I chided myself, because of course I did not know Corin Blackstone at all, and had no idea whether or not he would show such courtesy to me.

Sendra and I descended the stairs. I was still

dressed in one of my good gowns but had decided not to change, for I might as well be married in something lovely, even if it might end up getting ruined by the time the day was ended. And I saw that a priest had joined my father and Master Blackstone, was conversing with the two of them in low tones, although they fell silent as I approached.

Perhaps I flattered myself, but I thought I saw a spark of interest in Corin Blackstone's eyes as he looked on me, although almost at once it disappeared, and he only gave me a slight nod. Very well, if that was how he wished to play it, then I would be as cool and composed as he.

Even so, I could not entirely ignore the flutter in my stomach as the priest took his place on the lowest step of the dais, with Corin and I standing before him. My father moved slightly to one side, and Sendra took up an almost identical position opposite him. We would have no other witnesses; other than the five of us, the hall was empty. But that was all custom required, even though this spare setting was a far cry from the lavish ceremony I had imagined for myself, with flowers on all sides and silk hangings on the walls, and a gown finer than anything I'd worn before for my bridal day.

I had attended the weddings of my brothers,

and witnessed the ceremonies at many others, both friends and distant relations, and so the words the priest spoke were familiar enough to me. Still, even though I did not falter as I repeated the ancient vows, some part of me kept thinking that surely I must be asleep and suffering a terrible dream. Once or twice I had had nightmares of marrying someone I did not know, but always before I had awakened the next morning to realize that those awful dreams were merely that, and nothing more. Now, however, I knew that no such sweet morning would come to end this particular nightmare.

At last came the time to share the ritual kiss. I tilted my face up toward Corin Blackstone and forced myself to keep my eyes open, so I might look on the man I must now call husband. Oh, gods, this close, I could see how truly handsome he was, how long the lashes that encircled his dark eyes, how finely chiseled his nose and mouth.

And now that mouth was touching mine, but briefly, only the faintest whisper of a kiss before he drew away. Surely I should not have reacted to such a cursory caress, and yet for some reason, I experienced an odd thrill that seemed to move through my entire body, a new kind of heat I could not entirely explain. Of course it could not be love, for I did not know this man at all. Was this what all the books and poems meant when they spoke of desire? That emotion was often described as hot and fiery, and although I couldn't say that I was precisely on fire, the flush brought on by Corin's kiss did not subside immediately, but continued to pulse deep within me, awakening a need I had never felt before.

"It is done," the priest said. "You are now man and wife, Corin and Marenna Blackstone."

If we had had a true wedding, then that was the moment when all would have risen from their seats and cheered the newly wedded couple. As it was, my father only gave a curt nod, while Sendra fished a handkerchief from within her sleeve and dabbed at her eyes with it.

"The day is early yet," Corin said, "and so I thought we should be on the road as soon as possible. That way, we can cover as much ground as we are able to before nightfall."

I did not much like the sound of his plan, but I was provided no chance to protest, for my father replied at once, "Yes, that sounds like a very good idea." He gave me the briefest glance before adding, "There are several good inns within an afternoon's walk."

Walk? Was he mad? I looked from him to Corin and back again, and could see nothing in either of their expressions that told me they were sharing a joke. Yes, I had known I would have to go forth from this place with only what I might pack in one bag, but I had never thought that I would be forced to walk. Surely my father would not be so cruel as to make me go on foot, instead of sending us away with a pair of horses in addition to the fifty gold crowns he had already promised.

"But—" I began, but Master Blackstone cut in before I could continue, saying,

"And I do think it better if you change your gown, my lady wife. The road dust will ruin the skirts of that dress, and besides, it is best not to attract too much attention when traveling the high road."

"Very sensible," my father said. "Do go and change, Marenna, and be quick about it, so you do not leave your new husband waiting too long."

How could I even begin to protest? Yes, I understood the common sense of what Corin had just requested, and yet I hated the thought of having to go upstairs once again to put on something more suitable. It would have been easier if I could have simply walked away with my new husband. Now I would have to return to my bedchamber and be reminded yet again of everything I was about to lose.

Certainly I must have appeared crestfallen, for Sendra said quickly, "My lord, I will go up with her and help my lady change. It will not take very long at all."

My father didn't precisely smile, but something about his countenance seemed to soften as he looked down at my faithful lady's maid. "I thank you for your service, mistress. And fear not —your future will always be secure. I had a thought to send you to my son Evander's household, if that meets with your approval."

"It does, my lord," she replied, and sketched a hasty curtsey. "I very much appreciate your generosity. But now, let me do this one last service for her ladyship."

He inclined his head, and she bent and picked up my valise. Since it seemed any of my protests would be in vain, I said nothing, but only followed her back upstairs and stood in mute despair as she undid the lacing on my fine silken gown, then removed it and laid it on the bed. Luckily, the dress of dark green linen she helped me into after that had not been packed away long enough to acquire too many wrinkles.

Not that it matters, I told myself drearily, watching as Sendra took the silk gown and hung it in the wardrobe. *Soon enough this dress will lose its crispness, and its hem will be muddied and torn, and the best you can hope for is that you will not encounter anyone you might know as you travel the high road, for surely to see any of those fine lords and ladies when you yourself have been so cast down would be utter wretchedness.*

These terrible thoughts made tears sting in my eyes, but I blinked them back and took several deep breaths so they might help to push away the sobs that had begun to rise in my throat. The last thing I wanted was for my father to see how he had defeated me, or for my new husband to think I wept because I hated the thought of being married to him. Perhaps no one could fault me for feeling that way, but I knew I did not hate Corin. I did not know him well enough to hate him. Besides....

I thought again of the strange feelings his kiss had aroused in me, how my body had responded to him. No, that was certainly not hate. Possibly it could become the opposite, if he allowed it...and if I could ever learn to reconcile myself to this new and cruel life being thrust upon me.

Sendra passed the brush over my hair again, and then offered to braid it, since she said it would get dreadfully tangled being out in the wind and the elements. All I could do was nod, because I knew she had the right of the matter. In truth, as a newly married woman, I should put my hair up and not leave it lying loose like a maiden. But we certainly did not have time for the sorts of elaborate hairstyles I had seen the noble married ladies of my acquaintance wearing, and so the braid seemed like a passable solution.

Once Sendra was done, I thought I barely recognized my reflection—so wan and tense, with all the wealth of my long dark hair pulled severely back from my face. No jewels, either, for my maid had quietly suggested that I remove the gold and garnet earrings I wore, and the gold and pearl band on my right hand. No ring on my left, either, for of course my new husband had not seen fit to give me one. That lack made me feel as if I was not truly married at all, but I did not see what I could do about the situation. We were married in the eyes of the gods, and with that I would have to be content.

I descended the stairs once more, this time without the rustle of my silken skirts as accompaniment. And again my father and Corin Blackstone spoke in low tones, but left off as soon as I made my appearance.

"Much better," Corin said, giving me an

approving glance. My cheeks heated under his regard, but I did my best to stand there calmly and pretend as though there was nothing strange about the entire situation.

"Then you might as well be on your way," my father said. "Sendra, give her ladyship her valise."

Face tight with worry, the lines around her dark eyes seeming deeper than ever, my maid came to me and put the valise in my hand, wrapping my fingers around the handle—and placing her fingers on top of mine for the briefest moment, as though to offer me a final bit of encouragement. I could not exactly smile, but I nodded, hoping she would see in my eyes the gratitude I felt for her kindness.

Corin came to stand next to me, but I paused for a moment, and lifted my chin so I might look my father directly in the eyes as I spoke. "Goodbye, Father. I pray that someday you do not regret your rashness in this matter."

His stern expression did not waver. "Just as I wish the same for you, daughter."

I was already regretting my words to the Duke of Marric's Rest, regretting them a thousand times over, but there was little I could do about that now. I looked away from the man who had raised me, and into the dark eyes of the one who was now my husband.

"Let us go," I said clearly.

Corin put his hand on my elbow and guided me to the door. And so I left the only home I had ever known.

CHAPTER 3

We did not speak as we walked down the front steps, nor as we trod the long, winding pathway that cut through the castle grounds and the wall surrounding the keep. The sun was bright and cheerful overhead, seeming to care nothing for my current despair. Because we had had no rain for nearly a week, the roadside, once we reached it, was dry and hard and dusty. The slippers I wore allowed me to feel every pebble, every rut, but I would not complain, no matter how uncomfortable I might be.

That noble vow lasted for the first mile or so. After gritting my teeth and telling myself to ignore the pain for what felt like the thousandth time, I looked up at Corin and said, "I do not see why we could not have ridden. My father surely would have given you a horse, if you had but asked."

He shook his head. The fresh breeze had pulled a few strands of hair loose from the leather thong that bound it at the base of his neck, and they blew around his face now, dancing away as if happy to be so close to his handsome features. "Perhaps he would have," Corin replied. "But a horse is expensive to feed and look after, and we could not be guaranteed accommodations for one in any of the places where we might be going. It is better to walk and to be thus unencumbered."

Simple enough for you to say, I thought with some resentment as I looked at the sturdy boots he wore. They were made of thick brown leather, and had nice thick soles to match. No doubt he could not feel even a tenth of the same rocks and stones that had been biting into my feet. As for the rest, well, of course I had never needed to worry about how my father fed and sheltered his large stable of horses, or the packs of hounds he used in the hunt. I had taken my family's wealth for granted, like the sun rising every morning, or spring following winter. The silver in the mines behind my home seemed inexhaustible, and so of course were the funds that poured in to pay for the horses and my gowns and our servants and men-at-arms.

But I did have to admit that horses tended to eat a great deal, and were almost as particular as humans when it came to requiring a place to shelter for the night. However, I did not want to concede to Corin that he might be correct about the practicality of going on foot, and so I answered obliquely, leaving out any mention of horses but saying, "And where is it that we are going? Do you have some destination in mind?"

"Yes, that I do." His gaze shifted slightly to the southeast as he said, "We are traveling to Marric's Rest, for the vineyards there are extensive, and I believe I will have no trouble getting work during their harvest."

My heart seemed to stop at his words. No, he could not possibly be suggesting such a thing! To take me to the lands of the man I had scorned, to see everything that could have been mine, if only I had not been so impulsive! The only comfort I could take was that Corin did not know the true reason for my disgrace, only that my father wished to marry me off as quickly as possible.

And oh, gods, the ignominy if my path should ever cross that of Lord Sorthannic....

"There are no other estates in the vicinity that might offer the same work?" I asked, hoping that I sounded steady rather than ready to burst into tears, which was somewhat closer to how I felt in that moment.

"Not as many as you might think, for the lands here are newly come to the growing of grapes. It is a crop that fares better in warmer climes, but his Grace has been something of a pioneer in coaxing some very good vintages out of this rocky soil. I believe it is on his estate that we have the best chance of getting a situation."

Something about the way Corin's voice warmed as he spoke of growing the vines made me realize he must love his work. For some reason, that surprised me, for I had never given much thought as to whether the farmers on my family's own estates cared for what they did. It was their place in this world, just as it was mine to be the pampered daughter of the castle.

Not any longer, of course. Those days, it seemed, were already behind me.

"I see," I said. I knew there was no point in arguing with him, because of course he under-stood his prospects far better than I did. And really, the chances of my even seeing the lord of the manor had to be exceedingly slim. Unlike Corin, I would not be working in the fields. I assumed we would be given a cottage of some sort to live in, which I would manage. Exactly what taking care of our house might entail, I wasn't sure, but I assumed it would have something to do with cooking and cleaning...both fields of knowledge in which I was woefully lacking. I could embroider, and dance the *verdralle* with elegance and grace, and even prepare sweet sachets of herbs for a castle's wardrobes and clothes presses...all of which would do me very little good when it came to managing a household all by myself. Yes, I knew how to tell the cook to prepare a menu, and to inform a housekeeper that the chambermaids weren't getting into the corners as they should, but that sort of household was very different from the one in which I would soon find myself.

We walked in silence after that, a silence in which I increasingly had to fight to put one foot in front of the other, simply because every step had become more painful than the last. Surely Corin could not expect us to reach Marric's Rest by sundown; I had only a hazy idea of how far away it was, but I knew it had to be at least a day's ride, which meant two days on foot, if not more. But no, my father had mentioned that several inns lay within an afternoon's walk, so we could not be going quite that far.

At last I could not help myself, and allowed a whimper of pain to escape my lips. At once Corin paused and gazed down at me, his fine brows knitted with concern.

"What is it, Marenna?"

I drew in a shuddering breath. "I am sorry, but I cannot go a step further. My feet cannot manage it."

"Let me see."

In response, I lifted my dusty skirts ever so slightly, even as I told myself that it was not unseemly for Corin to see my ankles, for he was my husband. He knelt on the rough road and took one of my feet, lifting it so he could see the sole of my slipper. Truly, it was in far worse shape than even I had imagined, several holes already torn through the thin kid, dark blood staining its surface.

At once he assumed a most fearsome frown. "What fool sent you forth in such ridiculous shoes?"

"They are the only kind I have!" I burst out. "Or rather, I had some high boots for riding, but they would have been even more difficult to walk in, because of their heels—for catching in the stirrups, you know. At any rate, a lady does not tread the high road like a tramp, so I had nothing that would have been suitable for our travels today."

If anything, his frown deepened. "Are you saying that I am a tramp, my lady wife?"

Oh, dear. I realized then what a blunder I had made. Would my rash tongue ever stop getting me into trouble? "No, of course not," I replied. "All I am saying is that my former life did not prepare me for this sort of exercise."

The scowl lessened, ever so slightly. He shifted so he might look up at the angle of the sun in the sky, then glanced back down at me. "Well, we do not have so very far to go, for I had planned for us to stay at the inn in Oakfold. But it seems even a few more miles is more than you can manage at the moment."

"Oh, if it is only that far—" I began, trying to sound brave, rather than dismayed all over again at the thought of even walking a few yards, let alone miles.

"It is too far. But no matter. I will take care of you."

Before I could protest, his strong arms had gone around me, lifting me from the ground. I made a startled sound, pushing at the arms which held me, or at least attempting to, for I still carried my valise, which made things rather awkward. "You cannot mean to carry me for two whole miles!"

"Oh, yes, I very much mean to. Your feet are

already battered enough—you would be quite injured if you carried on as you have already."

As much as I wished to argue, I knew he had the right of it. Continuing to walk would only open new wounds on my feet. Besides, I had no way of knowing whether the injuries I had already suffered might not lead to infection. Gods, I hoped not. Not only would such an incapacity prevent Corin from reaching his destination, but I very much feared any doctor's fees would use up a good deal of the funds my father had given us.

"Very well," I said. "I am sorry."

"It is not entirely your fault. I should have asked to see what you were wearing on your feet before we embarked on this journey."

Should I tell him that he must not shoulder any of the blame in this matter? No, probably better to be silent and let him save his breath for carrying me. I was slender enough, but all the same, it could not have been easy to carry a grown young woman for several miles.

But he did manage it somehow, staggering into Oakfold just as the sun had begun to lower itself to the western horizon. It was a pleasant little village, with a well-manicured green at the center of town, and a stone well. Several of Oakfold's inhabitants stood at that well, drawing water. Our arrival piqued some interest, for at once one of the men came over to us, his dark eyes full of questions as he took in my husband and his curious burden.

"A mishap on the road?" the man asked. "We have not had any problems with bandits recently."

"Nothing so dire," Corin replied. "Just that my wife has injured her feet, and I thought it best to carry her the rest of the way into town. Can you give me the direction of your nearest inn?"

"Our *only* inn," the man said with a grin. He jerked his chin in the direction of a handsome two-story building, with brightly painted shutters at the windows and several horses tied up to the posts out front. "They'll take good care of you, though, and your wife." The man gave me a glance that managed to somehow be both pitying and admiring, and added, "Best of luck to you both."

Corin thanked the man, and turned and headed toward the building he had indicated. Almost as soon as we were inside, a stout woman of later years approached us, inquiring if I was quite all right.

"It's nothing that some rest couldn't mend," Corin said, and she gave a concerned nod.

"Of course, of course. I have a very nice room,

at the back of the house, quiet." The innkeeper—
for surely that was who the woman must be—
shot a worried look at Corin's face, adding, "It is
on the second floor. Do you think you can
manage?"

"It will be fine," he said calmly.

Whether or not it really would be fine, I
supposed I would discover soon enough. If it
turned out that he couldn't carry me up those
stairs, then I would simply have to go up them
under my own power. Yes, it would hurt, but now
that I had been off my feet for a few hours, I
thought I could manage.

However, he didn't seem terribly put off by
the burden he carried, and went up the stairs
with a far lighter foot than I could have managed.
The innkeeper led us down a narrow hallway,
then paused at the far end in front of the door on
the left.

"Here you are," she said. "It's two silver a
night, three if you want your meals brought up
to you."

"I think that might be best," Corin told her.
"And thank you—that's very generous of you."

She made an amused sound deep in her
throat. "I don't know about generous, good sir,
but it is an easy way to put some extra coins in
my pocket. Supper tonight is chicken stew and

fresh-baked bread, and will be served at the seventh hour."

A nod, and he said, "If you could also send up a basin of warm water?"

Her gaze flickered to me. "That's twenty-five copper *grauts*."

"It is no problem," he replied. "And thank you again."

She didn't precisely curtsey, but she did bob her head slightly, and promised that the water would be up shortly. Corin put his hand on the latch and lifted it, and entered the room that would be ours for the night.

While of course it could not hope to match the luxury I had left behind me, the space was pleasant enough, with whitewashed walls and dark beams overhead, and several chairs, a wardrobe, and a large bed with carved posts.

Seeing that bed made a flicker of unease awake within me. Yes, although I knew on some level that married couples generally occupied the same bed, I had not thought to apply that particular piece of wisdom to my own situation. But there was only one bed in this room, which meant Corin and I must occupy it.

I swallowed and told myself that at least it was early yet, and I wouldn't have to face that particular unpleasant reality for a few more hours. As it was, my husband seemed to pay no particular attention to the bed at all, and instead carried me over to the chair by the window, which looked down, not on some unpleasant alley, but a green little patch of grass, with a neatly kept stable off to one side. The innkeeper obviously made it her duty to provide fine accommodations for both her human and equine guests.

With an inner sigh of relief, I let go of the valise I had been clutching all this time and set it down on the floor next to the chair where Corin had placed me. At the same time, he hooked his thumbs under the straps of the leather pack he wore and eased it off his back, placing it on the floor next to my valise.

"Ah, that's better," he said, rubbing at his shoulder where the strap must have bitten into it. "I had thought I was traveling light, but—" He stopped himself there, as if he'd just realized that what he'd intended to say wasn't precisely polite.

Perhaps not, but true nonetheless. Corin was clearly a very strong man, but even his muscles must have been taxed after carrying me all that distance. However, I decided it was probably best that I not say anything, although I fixed what I hoped was an appropriately sympathetic expression on my face.

Luckily, a knock came at the door just then. Standing outside in the hallway was a boy probably a few years younger than I, a large green stoneware basin clutched in his hands. Next to him was a girl so similar in appearance—both of them with the innkeeper's bright black eyes and rosy cheeks—that I guessed they must be our hostess's children.

"Your water, sir," the boy said.

"You can put it on the table for now," Corin told him, and the boy did as requested, moving carefully so he wouldn't spill anything on the well-scrubbed wooden floor.

"And two mugs of cider for you and your wife, good sir," the girl put in pertly, her eyes curious and somehow avid as they took in my husband's tall form. "My mother thought you could use it, after spending all that time on those dusty roads."

For some reason, her inspection of Corin made me bristle. Terribly impertinent, I thought, and also quite inappropriate, since the girl didn't look to be much more than fifteen at the most. In that moment, I conveniently forgot how I had allowed myself to moon over some of my brother Evander's more attractive friends when I was around that same age. Still, I had known those young men to be unattached, whereas this chit obviously must realize that Corin was my husband.

"That was very kind of your mother," he said, taking the two heavy pewter mugs from her. "Do make sure to give her our thanks."

The boy, now relieved of his burden of the ewer of water, made an amused snort. "It's not kindness, sir. You'll be sure to find the sum on your bill, since drinks aren't included in the cost of your stay."

Corin's mouth quirked. "Well, I'll still see it as kindness, for I and my wife are quite thirsty. And thank you again."

Those last words made it clear he considered that to be the end of the matter, and that they should go. There was such an unmistakable note of command in his voice that neither of them seemed inclined to argue, and instead both took themselves off, although whispering to one another as they went, the girl sending one last longing look at Corin before he shut the door behind them, pushing it closed with his foot because both his hands were full.

"Your cider, my lady," he said, coming over to where I sat by the window so he might give one of the mugs to me.

"Thank you," I replied, and took it from him. The first tentative sip I took told me that the cider was very good, crisp and light and made from pears, rather than the apples I had expected. Until I swallowed the drink, I hadn't realized how thirsty I really was. Another sip, and the dust of the road began to be a memory.

Corin drank as well, a good long swallow that must have drained at least a third of the cider in his mug. Once he had satisfied his thirst, he set the mug down on the table and retrieved the basin of water, which he brought over to me and set down on the floor in front of my chair. "Now, let us see about those feet."

For some reason, those words sent a shiver through me. Perhaps it was only a fear of further pain; once I had sat down, the throbbing in my feet had retreated to the background, to be ignored while I focused on the comings and goings of the innkeeper's offspring. Or perhaps it was something much more than that. Although Corin had carried me for several miles, his arms around me the whole time, his touching my feet seemed a far more personal act. Unfortunately, I could not think of a way to stop him.

Instead, I sat there, teeth gritted against the coming pain—or simply the discomfort of such forced intimacy—as he took off my shoes, then undid the ribbon garters that held up my silk stockings and carefully eased them down my calves and over my feet. This time, I could not help but give a gasp of pain, for peeling away the stockings also took some dried blood with them, awakening those wounds once again.

"I am sorry," Corin said as he laid aside the shredded ruins of what had once been my second-best pair of silken hose.

"It's fine," I replied, my jaw still clenched. "It had to be done."

Without answering, he guided my feet into the basin of water. It was not hot, but nicely warm, and began to work on my injuries almost at once, soothing, gentle. Leaving me there for a moment, he went to his pack and pulled out a soft white cloth, then came back and knelt by the basin once again. After wetting one end of the cloth he held, he lifted my right foot from the water and began to dab at the burst blisters and outright cuts that had given me so much trouble.

A shiver went through me, although I wasn't sure it was because of the sharp, darting pains that flared up every time he touched an open wound, or simply because a man I hardly knew was kneeling there and holding my bare foot, his fingers warm against my flesh. It wasn't anything like desire, not like what had flared through my body when he gave me the marriage kiss, but something else, an acknowledgment that we were sharing even this casual intimacy.

"Tell me something of yourself, Corin," I said, thinking that perhaps distracting myself with conversation was the best way to survive his ministrations. "You work with vines, correct? Where did you learn such a skill?"

A small smile touched his lips, that slight lift telling me he knew exactly why I sought to fill up the silence with idle speech. "I am from Delanir to the south, about a day's ride from the capital. The grape and the vine were my father's vocation as well, and I learned from him until his death. But unfortunately, the man who employed my father and me, and who was kind enough to keep me on even after my father was gone, passed away some two years ago. His heirs did not wish to continue in the business, instead selling off the vineyards so they might have the cash in hand, and I was left to seek employment elsewhere."

"That sounds very cruel of them," I said. "One would think they might show some loyalty to those who had worked their vineyards, and to whom their own father had shown such kindness."

Corin shrugged. "To work with the vines—it is a calling, I think. For those who have no interest in such a thing, it can seem like an expensive and risky endeavor, since there is always the chance that a year's crop might fail, might be blighted by an early frost, or ruined by fungus if a summer is too damp. I cannot fault them for their decision."

Perhaps he was willing to be magnanimous, but I still thought it very wrong to treat loyal workers in such a way. My father had never let go a single person who worked in our fields, even on those occasions when frost or storm destroyed much of a hoped-for harvest. Then again, our true wealth came from the mines, not our farms, and so he could afford to take the long view in such things. Even so....

After setting my right foot back in the water to soak, Corin picked up the left and began to work on it as well. His fingers were gentle but strong, and I wondered if they were so deft because he had spent so many years working with vines, selecting the clusters to be harvested, carefully pruning as necessary to guarantee the best yield.

"And after that?" I asked, realizing a flush had risen to my cheeks as I watched him dab at the wounds on the sole of my foot, his eyes intent on his work.

"After that, I went to South Eredor and learned from some of the master vintners there. I had a little money given to me when I left my former post, enough to allow me to work my way to Eredor. I spent two years in the south, but I wanted to come home. Alas, employment is not as easy to find here as it was in Eredor, where they have made rather an art of winemaking. The climate there, of course, is much more conducive to such work."

I tilted my head slightly as I regarded this man who was now my husband. To be honest, I had never much thought about the wine in my cup as I took my nightly meals, except on those rare occasions when a bottle had gone bad. But clearly, it was Corin's passion, one that had taken him to far-off lands. I, who had never been farther afield than my family's town house in Iselfex, could not help but be slightly envious.

"So what were you doing near our estate?" I inquired then. "For certainly Silverhold has never had a reputation as a place of wine-making. I would have thought you would have gone directly to Marric's Rest, if the duke who resides there is as dedicated to the art as you say he is."

A lift of the shoulders, accompanied by a rueful grin. "I fear, my lady wife, that I was at Silverhold purely by accident. I had intended to go to Marric's Rest, but the directions I was given were sadly incorrect, and since I am not at all familiar with that part of the country, I did not know how off course I was until I came to your father's castle, thinking it the place I sought. He corrected me, and told me how I could journey to the duke's estate from there...but then he also told me of his daughter."

Corin paused there, and looked up from his work so his eyes might meet mine. Once again I felt that strange shiver move through my body, even though the room was warm enough.

"Yes, about that," I said, taking care to keep my tone light. "I must confess I find it rather odd that you would act on such an offer when you had no fixed home, and when you had not even laid eyes on the lady in question."

"No, I had not seen you," he admitted. "Not precisely, at any rate. But your father showed me your portrait where it hung in the hall, and so I knew you were comely enough."

Comely enough? I thought, a stab of irritation piercing me. *When the Earl of Ellesmere's son once said my beauty was enough to light up the heavens?*

At the time I had been flattered by those words, although in the end I had turned down his suit—mostly because I thought that having to spend the next fifty or so years listening to those sorts of fulsome compliments would slowly drive me mad.

Because I could not trust myself to reply, I remained silent, and after a moment, Corin continued with his story.

"Besides, I had been thinking for some time that I should find a place to settle, marry, have a family. I will be eight and twenty in a few months, far past the usual time when a man does such things. But I also wondered how I would find a wife, since my existence has been so unsettled of late." With gentle fingers, he put my foot back in the warm water, and set the cloth he had been using off to one side. I tried not to pay much attention to the rusty-colored stains that now marred the white surface of the linen. "So when your father made his offer to me, I thought it must be a sign from the gods, that here was the chance I had been looking for. Mad as it seemed, I could not help but accept."

How could I argue with such an argument? I supposed there were some who might question such unthinking acceptance of fate, but better that than agreeing to take me off my father's hands simply because fifty gold crowns was inducement enough for a man in Corin's position. I also reflected that I could have done far worse. At least the man who was now my husband was handsome and gentle and kind. He had carried me in his arms so I might take no further hurt, had washed my feet as tenderly and carefully as Sendra herself might have.

"But," he went on briskly, "we will have to see about purchasing you some real shoes tomorrow, and some thicker stockings, or you will be no better off than you were today."

While I could not question the wisdom of such purchases, I also couldn't help quailing at the thought of walking on feet that hadn't had a chance to heal properly. "Perhaps—perhaps we should stay here for a few days, make sure I am fit to travel before we worry about such things."

A line etched itself between his brows as he frowned. "No, I cannot afford that delay. Already I have lost time because of being sent in the wrong direction, and I dare not lose any more days. Otherwise, we risk appearing at Marric's Rest, only to find the bulk of the harvest done, and no work to be had. I will also buy some fresh linen to make bandages, and we will wrap your feet so you will suffer no further hurt."

How could I argue with him? I knew he spoke only the simple truth; although I had no intimate knowledge of the grape harvest, I knew enough about farming in general to understand that all crops had their days when they would be at their peak, and therefore best for harvesting. If I asked Corin to stay here, we ran the very real risk of not earning enough to get us through the winter.

"I suppose that should be all right," I said. My tone sounded grudging even to me, however, and I quickly added, "I am quite sure that a good night's rest will make me right as rain."

He smiled, although I thought I noted something strained about his expression. Almost as though against his will, his gaze flickered toward the sturdy bedstead set up against the opposite wall.

Oh, dear. I had nearly forgotten about that. Because I did not want to betray my own anxiety, I sought to change the subject. "My feet are feeling ever much better. Perhaps I should take them from the water now?"

"Yes, I think that will be fine." Corin waited as I pulled my feet from the basin—to be fair, the water within was now no more than lukewarm, and therefore not providing much of a service any longer—and then blotted them with the cloth. "I would let them dry in the air before putting on a fresh pair of stockings, though."

"Of course."

He stood, then said, not quite looking at me, "I will go downstairs and check to find out when we can expect our dinner. And I think I will ask for a bottle of wine. We should have something to celebrate our wedding."

I could only nod, thinking once again how different this reality was from what I had imagined for my wedding day. And then, once Corin had gone downstairs to speak with the innkeeper, I allowed a relieved breath to escape my lips. I needed a moment to myself, to collect my thoughts. Yes, I still had very little idea of what being married actually entailed, but I knew it must have something to do with the bed, which now seemed to loom larger and larger, like some frightening monster out of legend.

Unfortunately, there seemed to be little I could do to avoid my fate.

CHAPTER 4

"Not the most illustrious of vintages, I fear," Corin said as he poured some wine into my pewter goblet. "But somewhat more festive than mere cider."

"I am sure it will be fine." We sat at the table by the window, with the purple hour of dusk sending its soft, mysterious light into the chamber. Candles flickered in the sconces on the wall, and a squat specimen sat in a tin plate on the tabletop between us. Its light awoke new shadows and planes and contours in Corin's face, accenting the hollows beneath his cheekbones, the dark glitter of his eyes.

Although this was the same man who had brought me here earlier today, he seemed different in that light, even more of an unknown.

I told myself not to be overly dramatic, for in truth, his demeanor was friendly, almost casual, as if we were two friends meeting for a long-delayed meal, rather than a pair of newlyweds sharing their first supper.

He raised his cup. "To the most beautiful woman in the province."

Warm blood rushed to my cheeks. "Good sir, you need not be extravagant in your praise simply because I am now your wife."

"Oh, I do not think I am being extravagant." His head tilted to one side as he surveyed me, while I did my best not to flush even more than I already had. "No, you are exceedingly beautiful, Marenna Sedren."

"Marenna Blackstone," I corrected him gently.

"Ah, yes." He was silent for a moment before going on, "I do not think there is even a woman at court who could hold a candle to you. It is a pity that those fine ladies will not have a chance to be properly outshone."

His words puzzled me, for certainly he had not described to me a life where he had been anywhere near court. "Have you seen the court ladies?" I asked. "I did not think you had been to Iselfex."

At once he seemed to go still, and then he

shrugged slightly. "Oh, I have traveled many places, my lady wife. So yes, I have been to Iselfex, and had the honor of seeing his Majesty and his court ride out from the palace to take their sport in the countryside."

Oh, what a wonder that must have been. Right then, I could not quite hold back a flicker of resentment toward my father, who had never had much use for court, much preferring quiet life in the country. Indeed, after a trip to the capital when I was barely six, we had never returned. Our town house there retained a skeleton staff to make sure all was in order, just in case his lordship ever took the notion to visit Iselfex, but I knew my father would not do such a thing. And since one's presence at court was not a prerequisite for retaining one's title, I doubted he ever would.

"I have heard Her Majesty is very beautiful," I said. That was no more than the truth, for even in Silverhold we had heard the tales of our young Empress, how her hair flamed like fire—a rarity here in Sirlende, where almost everyone had dark eyes and hair—and how she had come from nothing to become the highest lady in the land.

"Yes, I suppose she is," Corin remarked, but his tone was so offhand that I could not feel any jealousy over such a comment. "But I still think you might surpass her."

"And the Crown Princess," I persisted. "I have also heard her beauty was such that lords and princes from all over the continent vied for her hand."

A strange, shuttered expression overtook Corin's features. He took a sip from the wine in his cup, and I followed suit, realizing that we had never properly finished our toast. After he sipped again, he said, "Well, of course her Highness would be in demand, for she was the sister of the Emperor. I very much doubt her beauty had a great deal to do with it. At any rate, despite what the stories might have said, there were not that many available to 'vie for her hand,' since most of those princes and lords had been promised from birth to someone else."

His tone was far harsher than I had yet heard it, and I wondered at his vitriol. But then I recalled how the Crown Princess had thrown over Lord Sorthannic to marry the Hierarch of Keshiaar, and wondered whether my new husband was experiencing some misplaced anger on behalf of the man he hoped would soon give him employment and a place to live. While I could not completely understand Corin's anger, I did think it would probably be better to make sure I did not mention Princess Lyarris after we reached Marric's Rest.

"Ah, I had not thought of it that way," I said, and set down my goblet so I might take up my spoon and get a bite of chicken stew, now that it had had a chance to cool down a bit.

For a moment, Corin did not speak. Then his expression grew gentle, and he asked, "Why were you not promised from birth, Marenna? As the daughter of a baron, should you not have had a betrothed?"

I was not empty-headed enough that I couldn't recognize a change of subject when I saw one. However, I was glad of the chance to speak of something else. "Yes, but my mother begged my father on her deathbed that I might be allowed to choose my own husband. Of course my father could not refuse such a request, and so I was left free." *Not that her pleas had the desired effect,* I thought, *for I still have ended up married to a man my father chose for me.*

It seemed that Corin was thinking much the same thing, for he said quietly, "I am sorry that choice was taken away from you. I had no idea."

All I could do was offer him a sad smile. "Oh, do not trouble yourself too much, Corin. I had been searching for a husband for the past year, and with little luck. Unfortunately, what my mother forgot to consider was that all the truly eligible young men would have been betrothed themselves. So perhaps you have the right of it in your belief that it was the gods who brought us together."

He put down his goblet and reached across the table so he could lay his hand on mine. Oh, how strong and warm his fingers were, how strangely reassuring! Once again I felt a tremor go through me, a need awakened by his touch, even one so gentle and friendly, with nothing of passion in it. "If that is the case, then I must make sure that I am a very good husband to you, for you deserve no less."

I was not so sure about that. While I was willing to concede that perhaps the gods had intervened when they brought Corin Blackstone to my father's estate, I wasn't sure they had done so by way of giving me any kind of a reward. I had been foolish and impulsive, and, if I allowed myself to pause and look back over my career as the daughter of the castle, I could only think of the many times when I had considered my own comfort and my own needs above those of anyone else. Some might say that was merely my due, as a consequence of my station and my birth...but now I did not know if I could agree with such sentiments.

"You have already been a good husband to me," I said lightly. "For you have carried me here, and tended to my feet. There are many who would have left me to my own devices or, at most, have asked the innkeeper to take care of me."

The corners of his mouth turned down, and his fingers rested on the handle of his spoon as he seemed to consider my words. "I would like to argue with you on that point," he replied. "Unfortunately, while travel can broaden the mind, it can also expose a person to some of the world's less desirable behavior. But I will continue to endeavor to do my best."

These words only made me smile at him, even as I found myself wondering at their elegance. While I had not spent much time around the laborers on our estate, or the people who worked the mines, I had seen and heard enough to know that they generally did not speak like someone I might have met in my father's audience hall. But then, the growing of grapes and the production of wine was a somewhat more exalted endeavor than growing barley or herding cows, and so most likely Corin must have spent a good deal of time around those with the means to engage in that sort of activity, and perhaps had absorbed something of their manner of speech. For all I knew, he had also learnt to read and write at the estate where he had grown to manhood. I thought it best not to ask, though, just in case he might not have been given those advantages, and was embarrassed by the lack.

"Marenna," he began, then paused, as though he was not quite certain of the words he planned to say next. His fingers tapped at the base of his goblet before he went on, "I think it best if we do not speak of your origins. They would only give rise to questions that I doubt either of us would wish to answer. Do you understand?"

What could I do but nod? For of course I had no desire to tell anyone of how I had been handed off to Corin. That would require an explanation for my father's behavior, and the revelation of how badly I had behaved to Lord Sorthannic. Besides, we would be living among humble folk, and I feared they would never accept me as one of their own if they knew that I was the daughter of a baron. "Of course, Corin," I said. "If asked, I will think of something that doesn't reveal anything of my true family or background."

The relief in his expression was clear. "Thank you, Marenna."

We were silent then, each of us eating the quite excellent chicken stew, thick with wine and mushrooms, and taking small sips from our goblets. It was not an awkward silence, though, and I thought that perhaps my father's rashness in sending me away with Corin Blackstone might have a happy ending after all. We would need time to get to know one another, to learn of each other's faults and strengths, and yet I thought in time we could become a true married couple.

And love? Well, it was early to cast a judgment on such a weighty topic, and yet, as I lifted my eyes from my bowl of stew so I might gaze on Corin's face, might study his features a little more closely, so that perhaps one day they would be as familiar as my own, I thought I might come to love him...if he would let me.

We finished our meals, and he took up the empty bowls and goblets and placed them on the tray the innkeeper's daughter had used to bring them to us. As I watched, he went to the door and opened it, and set the tray on the floor outside. Once the door had been closed and latched again, he offered me an uncertain smile.

"This must have been a long, strange day for you," he said. "It is probably best if you get some sleep."

All through dinner I had done my best not to look over at the bed, but now I had little choice. I glanced at it, then down to where my valise sat, still on the floor by the table. Sendra had packed several nightgowns for me, and so that was not the problem. No, it was simply that our room was only that—a single room, with no separate dressing room or bath where I might take off my linen dress and change into a nightgown. As easy as I had begun to feel with Corin, I did not think I was quite ready to do something so bold in front of him.

He spoke again, clearly noting my hesitation. "I will turn my back while you change out of your gown. There is no need for you to worry."

I thought that there was in fact a great deal to worry about, but I did not want to contradict him, especially since he had already turned his face toward the wall, his back to me. In a murmur, I said, "Thank you, Corin." And though it did hurt to get up from my chair and walk to the bed so I might retrieve my nightgown from the valise I had set there, I worked quickly, pulling out the garment in question, fingers fumbling with the fastenings of my gown. Thank the gods that this one had been constructed with side lacings, rather than lacing up the back, or I feared I might not have been able to get out of it at all, used as I was to having Sendra help me with such things.

At last, though, I was in my nightgown, and

had folded my dress and chemise and put them away. Padding carefully on my sore feet, I went to the bed and pulled the covers back, then climbed in. Hoping my voice didn't waver too much, I said, "I am ready."

Corin turned back toward me, face impassive. His gaze flickered briefly to the open neckline of my nightgown, and I could feel myself flush. In truth, the linen garment did not expose anything more than the gown I had worn that day, and yet it felt so much more intimate, illicit somehow. I had no idea what emotions my face betrayed in that moment, but it seemed he did not much like what he saw. Mouth tightening somewhat, he told me, "I shall sleep on the floor."

"But you cannot do that!" I protested, even while a flood of relief went over me. Until Corin had spoken, I hadn't realized how much I dreaded the notion of him lying down next to me. Yes, that was part of being husband and wife, I supposed, but it also would have made this whole situation real in a way I hadn't quite yet grasped. It was one thing to walk down the road together, or to share a meal—or even to have him wash my feet or carry me when I could no longer walk. But to share a bed with him....

"I think it is for the best," he said. "We are both very new to one another, after all. Besides,

you forget that I have traveled all over the continent, in far rougher conditions than this. Yes, the
floor might be hard, but I am indoors and warm,
and not sleeping in someone's haystack out
under the stars."

I hadn't considered such a thing. Perhaps this
was no real hardship for him, and yet I found
myself reluctant. Surely it would be very selfish
of me to expect my new husband to lie on the
floor while I had all the comfort of this feather
bed to myself. I took in a breath, then said, "No,
Corin. I cannot let you do that. This bed is very
large, with room for both of us. We have a long
way to walk tomorrow. Would you be able to do
that, with an ache in your back from sleeping on
the floor?"

He gave a reluctant chuckle. "You speak as
though I am a greybeard of seventy years, rather
than a man who has not yet reached thirty. I
think my back will fare well enough."

"But—"

"I will be fine," he cut in, his tone implacable.
"However, you may give me the coverlet to wrap
around myself. That will leave you the blanket,
and, as the night promises to be mild, I think you
will do well enough with only the one covering."

It seemed he was not to be argued with. Mere
stubbornness had never stopped me before,

although I was beginning to think that in Corin Blackstone, I had met my match. At any rate, it seemed foolish to keep protesting, especially since I knew deep down that I would do much better if I had the bed to myself. We had a long future as husband and wife ahead of us. What difference did one night make?

With a sigh, I lifted the coverlet and began to pull it away from me. Corin came to the bedstead and took hold of the heavy quilted linen, lifting it completely off the bed so he might tuck it under one arm. After that, he bent and blew out the candle on the bedside table. The tapers in their sconces and the short pillar on the table remained lit, but even losing that one candle was enough to make the room darker than I had expected, the corners alive with shivering shadows.

"Good night, Marenna," Corin said, and moved away from the bed so he could extinguish the rest of the candles. Full dark fell upon us, with only the faintest illumination from the slender moon that hung outside the chamber's east window.

"Good night, Corin," I replied.

Somehow I doubted either of us would spend a good night, though.

I awoke and blinked at the unfamiliar ceiling of whitewashed plaster and dark beams above me, so different from the carved and gilded ceiling in my bedchamber at Silverhold. From the floor on the other side of the bed came a faint groan, and all the events of the day before came rushing back to me—my father's wrath, the limping journey here to Oakfold...the man who was now my husband.

He sat up, brushing the hair out of his eyes. Although he had kept it tied back for the night— just as I had left my own hair confined to its braid, so it might not tangle too badly—some of his heavy dark locks had fallen away from the cord that bound them at the base of his neck. His head turned, and his dark eyes caught mine, somewhat sleepy but still very aware. "And how did you fare last night, Marenna?"

"Probably better than you, my husband."

A wide grin then, far bigger and brighter than it probably had any right to be. "Ah, I am not so sure about that. This coverlet was quite thick, and the room warm enough. It is better than I have had for the last fortnight."

I wasn't quite sure whether I should believe him, or whether he was teasing me. Although he had been dressed plainly when I first met him, his person had been clean and neat enough, and he looked nothing like someone who might have spent several weeks sleeping under trees or in hedgerows. "If you say so."

"I do." He stretched then; I could hear joints popping, but as he seemed more pleased by the sound than not, I refrained from making any comment.

"And so your plans for today?" I inquired, although I thought I knew the answer. Still, I couldn't quite prevent myself from hoping in my heart that perhaps he had changed his mind and had decided that it would be safe to remain here for another day. While my feet weren't currently giving me any particular twinges or throbs, I guessed they would have a different story to tell once I attempted to stand upon them.

One eyebrow lifted, but he appeared calm enough as he replied, "First, to obtain more suitable footwear for you, and then off to Marric's Rest. Even if we do not get on the road until late in the morning, we should be able to reach Lord Sorthannic's estate before dusk. It is not so very far—no more than twenty miles at the most."

Twenty miles. That sounded as far away as Keshiaar itself, but I did not protest. We had already settled on this plan the day before, so the time for arguments was past.

Corin pushed himself to his feet, and I immediately looked down at the blanket that covered me, in case he was not suitably covered. However, from the corner of my eye I could see that he was still fully clothed, had only taken off his suede vest and shoes, so my precautions turned out to be unnecessary. He went to his pack and got out a fresh shirt, then threw me a devilish look over one shoulder.

"You may wish to avert your eyes again, my lady wife."

I could not mistake that glance, nor the teasing note in his voice. But I did as he requested, because I was not sure I wanted to look on his bare torso. If a mere touch from him was enough to send my blood racing, what might seeing his partially clad body do?

He went on, "You may stay here and get dressed. I thought I would take one of your slippers with me so I might match the size at the local cobbler's, and hope he has something that will suit."

"That sounds like a good plan," I agreed, then shot a surreptitious look at him from under my eyelashes. By that point, he had already pulled on a new shirt, and there was not much to see.

Not sure whether I was disappointed or relieved, I went on, "Are we to have no breakfast?"

"I will inquire with the innkeeper when I go downstairs. I am used to not breaking my fast until lunch, except for perhaps having a bit of bread, but I assumed you would need something before we got on the road."

"That is very kind of you, Corin. Thank you."

He picked up his suede vest from where he had draped it over the back of a chair, and drew it on. "You'll need your strength for our walk today. It is nothing." After that, he bent and retrieved one of my slippers, which I had left at the foot of the bed when I changed into my night things the evening before. "I hope I shan't be too long."

I hoped not, either, but it seemed terribly forward for me to say such a thing. Instead, I nodded, and waited for him to go out and shut the door behind him. As soon as he was gone, I slipped out of bed and gingerly stood, testing my weight on my feet. They still ached, but I thought that if I had a good pair of sturdy shoes and some thick socks, I should be able to do well enough. Or rather, I hoped I should fare well. Twenty miles was a great distance, especially for someone not used to walking even a fraction of that length.

Still, I didn't have time to dwell on future

pain. Since I was blessedly alone, I needed to take advantage of this time to get dressed and prepare myself for the day as best I could. On most mornings, I would have had a hot bath, but it was clear no such luxuries would be forthcoming today. All I had was the basin of water I had used to soak my feet, and I shuddered at the thought of trying to bathe in that. I had to settle for finding a clean corner of the cloth Corin had used the day before to dab at my wounds, and very sparingly using some of the drinking water in the jug the innkeeper had left for us to wipe off my face and hands.

Then it was time to strip off my nightgown and put on a fresh chemise, and the other of my two linen dresses, since the one I had worn the day before was already dusty and stained. No doubt the one I put on now would suffer a similar fate, and I fretted over what I should do after that. Yes, I had the silken gown I'd been wearing when Corin came to my father's castle, since Sendra had packed it away for me, but it certainly was not suitable for walking the high road.

As I fastened the laces on my linen dress, I tried to reassure myself that the silk gown would do just fine once we reached our destination. We might not be living in luxury, but we would have four walls and a ceiling, and I would be done with foot travel.

And what if they turn you away? I fretted, fingers working to undo my braid so I might brush my hair and start over again. *Then you will be back on the road, and in a gown that will make you a likely target for thieves.*

No, that wouldn't happen. I wouldn't allow myself to believe that such a terrible outcome might be waiting for us. We would have a placid walk to Marric's Rest—a glance outside the window told me that the day was sunny and fine again, with only a few clouds in a bright blue sky —and then they would welcome Corin, glad to take on someone with such experience. We would be safe.

After that...well, we would just have to see. Certainly I could not envision a marriage where my husband spent every night sleeping on the floor.

I folded my nightgown and put it away, then fastened the buckle on my valise and went to set it on a chair. My feet twinged as I did so, and worry darted through me. If they hurt taking only a few steps, how on earth would I be able to manage twenty miles or more?

Someone knocked at the door. Would Corin be back that quickly?

Trying to keep from wincing, I hurried over to answer the knock. No, that was not Corin outside, but the innkeeper's daughter, a tray with bread and fruit and a nice thick slab of ham in her hands.

"Your husband said as you'd like some breakfast." The girl's gaze slipped toward the bed, which I hadn't bothered to make up. Back home, that task was something one of the chambermaids had done, since such chores were beneath Sendra's station as well. Corin had carelessly tossed the coverlet onto the foot of the bed, making the whole thing look more rumpled than ever. The girl gave me a knowing smile, although she didn't say anything else.

No doubt she thought that Corin and I had gotten up to...well, whatever it was that married couples got up to when they were in bed together. I knew I was blushing, but managed to calmly say, "Thank you."

"It's nothing. There'll be an extra two *grauts* on your bill to cover it."

"Which my husband will take care of when he returns," I said.

"Oh, no doubt. He looks like a straight-up one. Enjoy your breakfast." Then she went out and shut the door after her.

I stared at the closed door for a moment.

"Straight-up one" wasn't precisely in my vocabulary, but I assumed that the girl meant she thought Corin looked like an honest man.

He had certainly given me no indication that he was anything else. Some men might have joined me in bed, no matter what my wishes might have been, but he had been utterly respectful. I reflected that it very well might have been the gods who sent him into my life.

Since I didn't know when he would come back, I thought it best to eat quickly. The food was simple but tasty enough, and I was glad of it, since another long day stretched ahead of me. After I had finished everything on my plate, and drunk it down with some of the water from the pitcher, I got up to take the tray over to the door, just as Corin had the night before. Before I got there, however, I heard his voice.

"Marenna? Are you dressed?"

"Yes," I replied. "And I have just finished my breakfast. I was about to put the tray out."

"Splendid."

He opened the door then, and took the tray from my hands. However, because he did so, I could not help but notice that his own hands were empty.

"Were you not able to find any shoes?"

"I fear not. But," he went on quickly, obviously noting my crestfallen expression, "I have come up with an even better solution than that."

A carriage and a pair of horses? I thought, but of course did not voice the question aloud. "Better than a new pair of shoes?"

"Oh, yes," he replied. "A donkey."

"'A donkey'?" I repeated, my voice blank.

"Yes. You will be able to ride after all. This is such a small village, the cobbler here only repairs shoes or makes them as needed, but has no stock on hand. However, his brother, the miller, happened to have a donkey who needed a new home, and for only ten silver pieces."

Yes, riding a donkey would certainly save my feet—but oh, the ignominy of being seen on such a mount! I could only pray...once again...that we would not encounter anyone I knew. I did not know if I could bear such shame. "That sounds like an excellent bargain."

Corin paused then and peered down at me, as though to get a closer look at my face. "You do not seem very happy about it."

"No, I assure you, I think it's excellent news. Only...." My words trailed off as I considered the best way to continue.

"Only what?"

"Only I had thought that you did not want

the care and feeding of a horse, that it would not be practical for us in our current position."

His expression cleared. It seemed he had thought I might have a slightly different reason for my objections...which of course I did, but I was not about to disabuse him of that idea. Far better that he think I was only concerned because of what we should do with the donkey once we reached Marric's Rest.

"Well, for one thing, a donkey requires far less fodder than a horse, and tends to be sturdier. I had thought we would see if there was any use for one on Lord Sorthannic's estate. If not, I have no doubt that someone in the area would be willing to take it off our hands."

I could see how that might work. If Corin offered the donkey as an enticement to hire him for the remainder of the season, he might have a better chance at gaining employment with the duke. If not, well, there must be a farm nearby that could use one.

Mustering a smile, I said, "That seems like a splendid idea. I have already packed, so I suppose there is no need to linger here."

"No, none at all, for I have already settled our account with the innkeeper." Corin went to gather up his pack, slinging it over one shoulder, then took my valise in his left hand and offered me his right. "Let me help you downstairs."

I almost protested, told him that I was certainly recovered enough to descend the staircase on my own. But I did not want to sound rude...and also, even though I did not quite want to admit it to myself, I looked forward to putting my hand in his.

Which I did, finding some comfort in the strength of this fingers, and the steadiness with which he helped me descend the stairs. The innkeeper beamed at us and said she hoped we would easily pass the rest of our journey, while her daughter, who was standing by a shelf full of pewter mugs and polishing one of them, gave me another of those knowing glances, followed by a very obvious inspection of Corin's person, looking him up and down with a gleam in her eyes.

Luckily, my husband did not notice, or at least he affected not to. We went outside, where indeed waited a small donkey with a thick blanket on her back. No saddle, of course, but we should be going at a sedate enough pace that I hoped I would be able to manage. Corin helped me up onto my new mount and handed me my valise. I gripped it with one hand while I clutched the blanket with the other, and then we were off, the donkey's lead rope firmly in my husband's hand, his pack now resting on his shoulders.

The sun was warm on my back, the wind cool and fresh. Truly a lovely day, and yet...

...and yet I could not quite be happy, for I did not know what awaited us on Sorthannic Sedassa's estate.

CHAPTER 5

THE DONKEY DID NOT MAKE OUR JOURNEY ANY speedier, but it was far more comfortable for me. My abused feet, now tucked back in their worn slippers, felt better already, now that they had been given a few more hours to recover. And while the rough gait of my mount did tend to jar me, it was still a welcome alternative to having to trudge the weary miles.

I noted that the hills of my own ancestral home had given way to rolling plains, covered in rich farmland. The wheat and barley waved golden beneath the friendly sun of Sevendre, and we also passed groves of apples and pears, the branches of the trees heavy with fruit. Truly this land did seem friendly and abundant. No wonder Lord Sorthannic had decided to attempt growing grapevines here. Even though that crop had traditionally been confined to the southernmost parts of Sirlende, I saw no reason why it shouldn't prosper here as well.

However, lovely as the day might be, I could not help brooding over the master of the lands where we now traveled. I had tried to reassure myself that there was no reason why his path should cross with that of a common laborer, let alone the laborer's wife, but what if I was wrong? How could I possibly explain the way I had spurned him over something as foolish as an unkempt beard, but had no problem marrying a man far beneath my station?

I could not explain it, because, put that way, the situation made little sense. Yes, much of the blame for my current circumstances could be laid at my father's feet, but then again, if I had not been so heedless, he would have had no reason to be angry with me.

"There is a pretty little grove up ahead," Corin told me, swiveling his head slightly so he could look back over his shoulder. "It does not appear to be fenced in, so I thought it would make a good place to stop and have our luncheon."

"That sounds like a good idea," I replied, and glanced past him so I could see the grove he had mentioned. Yes, there was a stand of beech and elm, their leaves fluttering in the breeze, a patch here and there of gold and amber telling me that they would soon be putting on their autumn colors. I did not mention that my backside was beginning to feel quite sore from jouncing up and down on the donkey's bony spine, for that would make it sound as if I would not be content with any mode of transportation that did not involve a couch and four. Inwardly, I believed that to be the case, but I kept my thoughts to myself. No doubt Corin already thought me spoiled and sheltered enough.

We came to the little grove, and he tied the donkey's lead rope to one of the slender beech trees, although loosely enough that the animal would be able to reach the grass growing around the base of the tree. Once Corin was finished with that task, he slipped out of his pack and set it on the ground, and at last reached over to help me off the donkey's back.

It did feel good to stand again, to stretch and work some of the stiffness out of my legs and back. And although I only wore my battered slippers, the grass underfoot was soft and springy, and posed no hardship at all.

Corin took the blanket from the donkey and spread it on the ground. "Your seat, my lady."

I carefully eased myself onto the blanket and took in a deep breath of the sweet, fresh-smelling air. "It is quite lovely here."

"I am glad you like it." He went back over to his pack and extracted several packets wrapped in muslin. "The innkeeper sent bread and cheese along with us, and a few slices of bacon. Cold, of course, but I've found that matters little when one has sufficient appetite."

"It sounds lovely," I said. Polite, empty words, for of course I would have far preferred a slice of hot meat pie. However, I was hungry enough that even the rough rations Corin had mentioned would do in a pinch.

He came and sat down across from me on the blanket, and unwrapped one of the packets, revealing a chunk of blue-veined cheese. The next contained a whole loaf of bread with a pleasing golden crust, as well as the slices of bacon he'd promised. There were only four, but they were quite thick and nicely browned, so they should do very well.

"We are making good time," he said as he doled out the bread and cheese, along with the bacon. I could not help but notice that he gave me larger portions, even though I had had breakfast, while he went without. Pointing this out to him did not seem like a good idea, and so I resolved to eat daintily and insist that he finish what I could not. That way he could at least have his hunger somewhat satisfied and still feel as though he had shown me the courtesy he clearly thought due his wife.

"Are we?" I inquired, after nibbling at some bread and cheese. "I must confess that I don't know this part of the country well, so I do not have a very good idea of our progress."

"I am not all that familiar with it, either, but we passed a mile marker a little ways back that indicated we only had seven miles to go until we reach Elmcroft, which is the village nearest Lord Sorthannic's estate." He picked up one of his pieces of bacon and broke it in half, then took a bite. As he lifted the bacon to his mouth, the sunlight flashed on a silver ring he wore on the little finger of his right hand.

I had noticed the ring before, but only in a cursory way, taking note of its presence without seeing any of its details. It was a handsome piece, thick silver in one of the complex twistwork patterns so beloved here in Sirlende, although unadorned by any stones. "That is quite a fine ring," I commented, then worried whether my tone had sounded at all accusatory, as though I had made the remark because I did not believe someone of his station should have something so expensive in his possession.

Corin glanced down at the band on his finger. "Thank you. It belonged to my father—a gift from the man who employed him. When he passed, it came to me. In truth, I sometimes fear that it makes me a target for thieves, but I look on it rather as a good luck piece and would rather wear it than keep it tucked away in a pouch or pocket."

"Ah," I said. Well, that explained why he owned what was obviously an expensive piece of jewelry. "Do you wear it when you work as well?"

"Oh, no," he replied at once. "I tie it to a leather thong and hang it around my neck. That way, I can keep the luck with me and not have to worry about losing it whilst working in the fields."

I nodded, and took a few more bites of bread and cheese. To tell the truth, looking at his ring only saddened me, for I could not help but think of all the fine jewels I had left behind in my father's home. It angered me that I could not have brought along even the simplest pair of silver earrings, but my father's will had been absolute in the matter. Corin and I could have sold those pieces, vastly supplementing the fifty gold crowns that were to be my only dowry.

A silence stretched between us, one I was not sure how to fill. Yes, I could not deny that I enjoyed Corin's company, or that his mere presence was enough to send delicious little flickers of excitement through my body, and yet at the same time, I vehemently wished that his situation had been different. I had not been born to travel the roads on the back of a donkey, or to sit on a blanket and eat bread and cheese like a peasant. Why, I did not have even the plainest of silver bands on my finger to show that Corin was truly my husband.

"I am sorry," he said quietly, and I looked up, startled, to see him watching me with a certain sorrow in his eyes.

"Sorry for what?" I asked. "The food is nourishing, and the setting here is beautiful. Whatever are you apologizing for?"

"For not giving you a ring to wear." He hesitated, his fingers twisting the ring he wore.

Surely he couldn't think I expected him to give me that one keepsake from his father? While I would admit that having a wedding band might have made our marriage feel more legitimate, I would never ask him to give up something that was so obviously precious to him. "It doesn't matter, Corin. And please, do not even think of giving me your ring. While I might appreciate the sentiment, I fear that heavy band would slide off even my largest finger. I could not bear to take away the only thing you have from your father."

He was silent for a moment, expression surprised and relieved at the same time. "You have a generous heart, Marenna."

"Oh, I am not so sure about that," I protested. Indeed, his compliment made me feel rather shamefaced, for I was not sure I had earned the praise at all. It was easy to be generous when one's family wealth allowed a person to be extravagant. Now I had nothing and could not quite keep myself from bemoaning that fact. I doubted that Corin would think me so generous if he had been able to see inside my mind, see some of the resentments I had just barely prevented from bubbling up to my lips. "I just know that I would feel dreadful if something were to happen to the ring your father left you. Perhaps—perhaps if all goes well at Lord Sorthannic's estate, and he pays you well enough, you can get me a ring. My birthday is at the end of next month."

"It is?" He smiled then. "That gives me a goal to work toward."

Indeed, he looked so pleased that I wondered if I should have kept silent about my birthday. It was not an event I looked forward to with any real enthusiasm. How could I, when in the past my father had always held grand celebrations in my honor, with families coming from all around to dine and dance and listen to the musicians he hired for the event?

I somehow doubted I would have anything quite so fine when my twentieth birthday came around a month from now.

"But if you have finished," Corin went on, his tone now brisk, "then we should get back on the road. I do not want to tarry here so long that we arrive after sunset."

"Oh, yes, I've finished." It had been a meager enough meal, one that could be quickly eaten. And he was right—I had only the haziest of ideas as to how one appeared at a noble's estate and asked for work, but I doubted it was the sort of endeavor that could be successfully accomplished after nightfall.

So I got up from the blanket, and Corin picked up the muslin that had wrapped our food and stuffed it in his pack. The blanket went back on the donkey, who did not appear all that happy to be interrupted in her grass-eating to have a human placed once more on her back. However, she was a sweet-tempered little creature and did not put up any fuss, but rather submitted to being led back out on the road so we could continue our progress.

Now the road began to be somewhat more crowded; we passed wains filled with sweet-smelling straw, or loads of apples, or barrels that might have been cider or wine or beer. A shepherd went past, a bright-eyed dog helping to keep his flock headed down the hard-packed dirt road, rather than wandering off into the fields on either side. Corin and I earned a few curious glances, but no one stopped to ask our business, and I saw no one who looked remotely familiar, which certainly helped to lift my spirits.

At length the sun began to dip toward the west, and the traffic lightened somewhat. We came to a crossroads, one with "Marric's Rest" neatly painted on the signpost there, along with an arrow pointing toward the east. If we continued on our current path, we would arrive at Elmcroft, but of course that was not our intended destination.

"Not so very long now," Corin said.

He had smiled, but it seemed to me that he now looked somewhat anxious for the first time, as if he was not quite sure of our reception at Lord Sorthannic's estate. True, if we were turned away, we still had money in our pocket, and certainly we should be able to find lodging in

Elmcroft without too much difficulty, but that would do nothing to solve the long-term problem of where we would live, of how Corin could earn a living.

I told myself that borrowing trouble never did anyone any good, and that of course a person with my husband's talents should be welcomed at Lord Sorthannic's estate. At the same time, I had to pray that his Grace would be occupied elsewhere, and not consulting with his overseer, for otherwise this would be a most awkward meeting.

The road took us to lands bordered by a low stone wall, a wall with an iron gate more for show than anything else, for it certainly was not tall enough to be defensible. Of course, Sirlende had not been at war for centuries now, and many estates—my father's included—had dispensed with the sorts of barricades that might keep marauders at bay. However, this gate was guarded by a pair of men wearing black and silver livery, with long swords at their hips, although they made no move to pull those swords from their sheaths as we approached. Then again, I supposed that a woman on a donkey and a single unarmed man were not quite enough to be any cause for alarm.

One of the guards stepped forward. He

looked to be a few years older than Corin, and although he seemed to be doing his best to appear stern, I couldn't help but notice a certain twinkle in his dark eyes as he looked the two of us over, his gaze lingering on me for a second or two longer than was strictly proper.

"State your business at Marric's Rest."

"I am Corin Blackstone, and this is my wife Marenna. I have come here because my experience is in the cultivation of vineyards, and I have heard that his Grace has extensive vines. I thought I would come to offer my services with the harvest."

The guard looked back at his companion, who also appeared to be in his early thirties, although his expression was far more forbidding. He frowned and scratched at the stubble on his chin, and appeared to be considering Corin's words without any real enthusiasm. Watching him, my heart sank. What if they turned us away?

But then he shrugged, and said, "I have heard they are in need of help, for the under-overseer fell and broke his leg last week. We will take you to see Master Brinsell, the overseer."

The dark clouds that had begun to gather above my head seemed to melt away at this pronouncement. Not that I wished the under-overseer—whoever he might be—any ill luck, but if he had to break his leg, his timing was certainly fortuitous.

"Thank you very much, good sir," Corin said. "I appreciate the opportunity."

The second guard lifted his shoulders again. The first guard, who was somewhat taller, bent and murmured something to him, although I could not catch what he said. Whatever it was, it seemed to amuse the other man, for a fleeting smile touched his mouth before he grew stern again.

"This way," he said as the first guard opened the gate.

Corin led the donkey inside, following the guard as he took us down a well-groomed path— well, a small road, really, certainly large enough to accommodate two wagons or carriages riding side by side—that cut through equally well-tended fields. Off to our left was acre upon acre of wheat, now turning even more golden in the light of the westering sun, while off to our right were the estate's storied vines, lush and lovingly cared for, their thick leaves allowing only tantalizing glimpses of the deep purple or pale green fruit hidden within.

Up ahead was the duke's castle itself, turreted towers reaching up toward the sky, flags in the silver and black of the household flapping in the breeze. The place was very much grander than the castle where I had grown up, and once again I could not help but scold myself, knowing that if I had simply learned to govern my tongue, I might have been mistress of all this magnificence.

Our destination was not the castle, however. The road forked, taking us off to the right, to a small settlement of a dozen or so cottages surrounded by trees, with a larger house of two stories set slightly back from the cottages and surrounded by more elm and beech trees.

It was to this house that the guard led us. "This is Master Brinsell's home," he explained. "I know he is back from riding the fields, for Ollin and I spied him heading home not a half hour earlier. You may go to him and plead your case."

Once again that nervous flutter started somewhere in my belly, for while it seemed that fortune might have smiled on us—as it certainly had not for the hapless under-overseer with his broken leg—I could not be certain of our fate until Corin spoke with this Master Brinsell. My husband, if he was experiencing any uncertainty, showed no sign of it; his chin was up, his shoulders squared, as though he was already going over in his mind everything he might say to his possible employer.

We stopped next to the two-story house, and Corin came to me and helped me down from the donkey. This time, my feet barely hurt, and I quietly blessed him for securing that unlikely mount, as I knew that even in sturdy shoes, I should have been in a good deal of pain if I had been forced to walk again today.

"I shall go in and announce you," the guard told us. "Wait here." He knocked once, said, "It is Cale," and let himself in without any more ceremony than that.

I cocked an eyebrow at Corin, and he smiled down at me. "It seems they are not too formal here, even if this is a grand estate. A good sign, I think."

"Let us hope so."

The guard emerged and said, holding the door open for us, "Master Brinsell will speak with you now."

We nodded in acknowledgment and went inside. Although of course this house was nothing like the castle of my birth, it appeared very snug and neat to me, with its whitewashed walls and dark-beamed ceilings and windows of diamond-paned glass. On one wall was a large cabinet that displayed an impressive collection of pewter goblets and mugs, and on another hung a painting of the estate itself, with the vines filling the foreground and the castle golden and magnificent in the background.

Sitting in front of the painting was a quite handsome man in his late fifties, or perhaps his early sixties. His grey-streaked black hair, which was still quite thick, had been pulled back from his face into a long tail not unlike the one Corin wore, and he had a closely trimmed beard with none of the betraying grey of his hair. He sat up a little straighter as the two of us approached and fixed my husband with a keen dark eye.

"So you know something of the vines, Master Blackstone? And where did you acquire this knowledge?"

"Sir, I learned it from working the fields in Delanir with my father, who was the overseer of an estate there. I had hoped to take over his duties after he left this world, but unfortunately, the owner of the vineyards passed away not so long after that, and his heirs sought to sell his land. That is why I must now seek employment elsewhere."

Master Brinsell listened to this narrative and nodded. "Well, your timing is fortuitous, for my right-hand man has injured himself, and he cannot walk the fields to perform the necessary inspections." His head tilted slightly as he looked up at Corin. "Is your knowledge confined only to growing the grapes, or to making wine as well?"

"I've assisted in the production of five vintages so far. They all did very well, with all the stock purchased by the wine merchants of Iselfex at a good price."

"Excellent." The older man rose to his feet; standing, he was only an inch or so shorter than Corin. "We will definitely have need of you during the harvest, and then we shall see how we stand. Am I to assume that you and your wife have need of accommodation while you work here at Marric's Rest?"

"Yes, sir, if any is available."

"As it turns out, we do have an empty cottage, although it needs a good airing-out." This time, Master Brinsell turned his attention to me, and gave me a quick glance up and down. Perhaps he was trying to assess my aptitude for performing such homely chores. I could only hope that such talent was not easily discernible by the naked eye, or he certainly would know that I was ill-suited for such a task. "The pay is forty silver for a week's worth of work, along with the use of a cottage. I can guarantee at least four weeks for you, possibly more."

It seemed like a piddly sum to me, but Corin

did not appear at all put off by the amount the estate's overseer had mentioned. "That sounds most excellent, Master Brinsell."

"Very good. Let me show you to the cottage, and you can get settled before sundown. Each of our workers is given an allotment of food supplies each week as part of their pay—I'll see that someone from the storerooms at the castle brings it down to you."

"That's very generous of you."

The overseer gave a deprecating chuckle. "Ah, well, we grow most everything here on the estate, so it is not too much of an effort to make sure everyone gets their fair share. If you'll come with me."

He began to walk to the door. I noticed that he had something of a limp and tended to favor his left leg. An injury, or was he merely suffering from the joint aches that often afflicted those of a certain age?

Of course I did not know him well enough to ask, and so I followed him and Corin outside, where my husband took the donkey by her lead rope.

"There is a corral where you can put your animal," Master Brinsell offered. "It is on the way."

I was relieved to hear that we would be able

to give the donkey a safe place to forage—and also happy to know that she would not be underfoot in our new home, like an oversized dog. Although such practices were very rare in Sirlende, I had heard in the far north some of the tribes brought their horses inside to live with them, and indeed treated the animals like members of the family. While I had to admit that the donkey had proved to be a steady and faithful mount, it did not mean I wanted her in my dining room.

Not that the cottage we were to be given probably had anything as grand as a dining room. We would be lucky to have an alcove with a small table and a few chairs.

Then I chided myself, for I knew we were lucky indeed, that Marric's Rest would have an opening for Corin, and that we would have a place to live, and food on our table. True, if I were the one responsible for preparing that food, our meals might not be the most edible, but....

We came to a corral where several sturdy-looking horses cropped at the grass within. Master Brinsell opened the gate, and Corin took off the donkey's lead rope so she might go in and join them. None of the horses appeared terribly bothered by this new arrival, which I hoped was a good sign.

Our livestock thus disposed of, we continued along a path that led past the cottages I had spied earlier, all of them appearing well-tended, with tightly thatched roofs and fresh whitewash on their walls, some with bright flowers still blooming from their window boxes. Perhaps Lord Sorthannic did not worry overmuch about his own grooming, but he certainly seemed to make sure that the people who worked his lands were well taken care of.

At the end of the path was a cottage that stood a little ways off from the others, with trees clustered around and open fields stretching beyond it. By that point, the sun was only a handspan above the horizon, and the entire scene was flooded with a warm, mellow light. Something tense and fragile within me suddenly seemed eased, as though seeing our destination and realizing it was nothing to fear had released a knot of worry I hadn't even realized I was carrying.

"Here you are," Master Brinsell said as he opened the door. "No one has lived here these six months, for Halic Trensly and his family, who were the previous occupants, left for the capital when his father passed on and left him a tidy sum. They left it in good enough repair, but it will still need some tending-to."

"That will not be a problem," Corin replied at once. "My lady wife and I will put it right in no time."

"I have no doubt you will." A small smile touched the corner of the overseer's mouth, but then he appeared sober enough as he added, "We will be going into the fields at first light. Meet me at the corral, and we will head out from there."

"I'll be ready."

"I have no doubt of it." Master Brinsell's gaze moved to me, and he nodded. "A very good evening to you, Mistress Blackstone. I will see that some prepared food is sent over, so you will not have to attempt to make dinner while you're tidying the cottage. In the morning, you shall also have your week's allotment of supplies."

"That is very good of you, sir," I said, relieved beyond measure that I would not have to prepare any food this evening. Yes, it was only one night's reprieve, but better than nothing.

"Then I will leave you to get settled. Have a very good evening."

He closed the door behind him, leaving Corin and me alone in our new home. I glanced around, noting that there was a good-sized room with a stone fireplace at one end, and an alcove not really large enough to fit the round table and four hard-backed chairs that had been set there. An opening in one wall showed a bit of the kitchen, with another hearth and counters of bleached wood, while a short corridor opened off the opposite wall, presumably leading to the bedroom, or bedrooms. It had been difficult for me to accurately gauge how large the cottage actually was just from looking at its exterior.

The place did seem sturdy enough, with real glass in the windows and a good roof, but there was dust everywhere, and cobwebs in all the corners.

"I'll look in the kitchen for a broom and some rags," Corin offered, perhaps noticing that I did not appear quite as pleased with my new home as I might be.

"Yes, I suppose we should get started on that," I said. Even though my enthusiasm for house-cleaning was somewhat lower than my desire to cook our meals, I knew I had to try to help. I would be no bargain at all as a wife if I did not at least give the appearance of domesticity.

"Why don't you look at the rest of the place first?" he asked, then eased the pack of his shoulders. "Here, take this and your valise, and find the bedrooms."

I noted that he used the plural, although I thought that might have been more due to wishful thinking than any true knowledge. Still, I supposed I should go find out. I took the valise with one hand and his pack with the other, trying my best not to stagger under the weight of it. How on earth he walked so many miles carrying something so heavy?

Giving him a nod of acquiescence, I took our luggage and went down the short hallway I had spied earlier. Yes, it seemed there were two rooms on this side of the house, one of them a good bit larger than the other, and with a sturdy wooden bed and a wardrobe up against one wall. In a corner was a basin for washing-up, and a largish window hung with muslin curtains took up another wall.

I set my valise and Corin's pack down on the wooden floor, and went to open the wardrobe. Inside were stacked sheets and blankets, leading me to wonder how much of their belongings the cottage's previous occupants had taken with them. Or perhaps the bedding came with the house, and so they had been compelled to leave it behind.

The smaller room contained two narrow beds, with a plain table between them. No wardrobe here, although there was a small chest set under the window. Clearly, this had been the children's room.

And perhaps now it should be yours, I thought. *With two bedrooms, there is no need for poor Corin to take his place on the floor. These beds are far too small for him, but you should fit well enough.*

But...certainly I would be doing him a disservice to insist on separate rooms. We were husband and wife, after all, and I might as well face up to the situation.

I turned around and saw Corin standing there, a broom in one hand and a folded white cloth in the other. "I thought perhaps if you dusted and I swept, we should make short work of the place."

"That sounds like a good idea," I said, taking the cloth from him. True, I had never dusted anything in my life, but how difficult could it be? I had seen the maids go about the castle with their cleaning cloths, wiping down everything in sight, and once a month using beeswax to awake a warm glow from within the carved wooden furniture. Somehow I doubted there was any beeswax here, but at least I could get rid of the dust. As best I could, I pushed aside the resentment which rose in me then, that I should be reduced to doing the kind of work that had been relegated to Silverhold's chambermaids. No matter what my personal feelings on the subject might be, it certainly would not be fair to expect Corin to perform all the work. "Let us do the main room first, since we don't know when our food will be arriving."

He nodded, and we went out to the living chamber, where I ran the cloth I held over the dusty furniture, and along the windowsill, while Corin used his broom to knock down the spiderwebs and then clear the debris from the floor. No doubt the cottage's wooden floors could also do with a good mopping, but that would have to wait until the next day. Or possibly longer than that. I somehow doubted that I would enjoy cleaning the floors any more than I liked dusting the furniture.

Partway through this work, my feet did begin to ache again, but I ignored them, knowing that this task had to be accomplished before we retired for the evening. The light grew dimmer, and Corin paused to fetch several beeswax tapers from a kitchen drawer, along with a wooden box of matches. Perhaps I had been wrong about the beeswax, then. I had been expecting tallow candles, for they were so much less dear, but possibly Lord Sorthannic also raised bees on his estate and shared the wax with his tenants. At any rate, the candles' illumination warmed the place, making the cottage feel as if it might one day be home.

We were just finishing up when someone knocked at the door. Corin went to answer that knock, the open door revealing a young boy probably no more than twelve, carrying a basket that seemed almost as big as he was.

"From the kitchen at the castle, sir," he said, handing the basket over to Corin. "Your supper, and some cold pie for breakfast tomorrow."

"My thanks to Master Brinsell, and to the cook."

The boy grinned. "Can't have our new under-overseer starve, can we? A very good night to you, sir."

Then he scampered off, as I stared at Corin in surprise. "'New under-overseer'? I thought you had only been brought on as an extra hand in the fields."

"So had I," he said, with a grin as bright as the boy's own. "I think our luck is changing."

"I hope so," I replied.

Gods, did I hope so.

CHAPTER 6

We had a merry dinner that night, for, as promised, we had been sent a hearty meal of chicken in a deep wine sauce with root vegetables, butter and a loaf of fresh bread, and a bottle of the estate's wine, along with the promised cold chicken pie for breakfast. Corin and I sat on our newly dusted chairs in the little alcove off the living chamber, and toasted each other with the quite excellent wine.

"To our future," he said, and I clanked my stoneware goblet against his. Luckily, the kitchen had been fully stocked with plates and cutlery and drink ware, so we lacked for nothing to make our meal a pleasant one.

"To our future," I echoed, then drank. Yes, it seemed that Lord Sorthannic—or at least his overseer—knew something about making good wine. It was rich yet smooth, tasting of fruit without being sweet at all. It went so well with the chicken dish we had been sent, I wondered whether some of it had been used to make the sauce...although that seemed rather like a waste of fine wine.

"If I acquit myself well, then perhaps I will be able to stay on after the four weeks Master Brinsell promised me are done," Corin went on. His dark eyes shone in the candlelight, and once again I thought how handsome he was, how any woman who looked upon him must think me lucky to be his wife.

And yet there I had been, contemplating sleeping in the children's bedroom.

"Is there a great deal of work to be done when one makes wine?" I inquired.

He chuckled. "Oh, yes. We have come here at harvest, which means first the grapes must be plucked before there is any danger of the first frost. The grapes are stored in large bins, but then they must be crushed and the juice drained away, and put in vats to begin the fermentation process. Later, the young wine will be moved to barrels, and yeast will be added to continue the fermentation. After it has aged for a year—or possibly longer, as I do not yet know how long this estate barrel-ages its wines—then it will be decanted into bottles. And all along it must be tested, and tasted, to make sure that it is developing in a pleasing manner."

"Goodness," I said, somewhat shocked at the intricacy of the process. "No wonder you hope to stay on much longer. It sounds as though your skills would be needed here year-'round."

"That is my hope. While I do not wish ill on anyone, I would be lying to you if I did not say that I rather hope the under-overseer will decide this work is not for him and will take himself off to better pastures, perhaps where he will not have to worry about breaking a leg again."

How could I fault Corin for thinking such a thing, when much the same notion had entered my mind as well? Yes, forty silver coins each week was not precisely a princely amount, but it should add up quickly enough, since our housing and our food would be provided for us. We had indeed come to a safe haven...now all we had to do was hope it would last.

And that my path would not cross Lord Sorthannic's. I thought the chances of such an eventuality were rather small, for I did not believe his Grace would have much reason to come down here to this settlement where his workers lived, and certainly there would be no reason for me to go up to the castle. My place would be here, in this cottage—keeping it neat and clean.

And trying to learn how to cook so I do not poison the both of us, I thought with some trepidation. Since I had not set foot in my own home's kitchen since I was child—and only then to steal cookies—I did not expect to have much success in such an endeavor. However, I would have to try. Corin would have much the worse of the situation, since he would have to be up before dawn every day to ensure the grape harvest was brought safely in.

"That would be the best outcome," I agreed, and took another bite of chicken in wine sauce. If this dish was any indication, the cook in Lord Sorthannic's castle was very good, even better than Linsey, who had presided over the kitchen in my father's castle ever since I could remember. But then, of course the duke would have an outstanding cook. He was one of the peers of the land, of such rank that the Emperor himself might come here for a visit.

Or would he? I could not help but think that relations must be strained between them, what with the Crown Princess throwing over Lord Sorthannic to sail off to Keshiaar and marry that land's ruler.

At any rate, I found myself wishing that every evening could be like this, with a basket of delectable dishes delivered to our door...and with as little time spent in the kitchen as possible.

"You seem rather pensive, my lady," Corin said. His fingers were wrapped around the thick stem of his goblet, but he did not appear inclined to lift it to his lips to take a drink.

"Oh, I suppose I am only trying to adjust to all these alterations," I replied. "For remember, just yesterday morning, I awakened in my own bed in my father's castle, and had no thought that my life was about to change forever. It is all rather much to take in—being here, away from everything I have known, realizing that this is my home." *For now, anyway,* I added mentally. It was good to hope, of course, but we had no concrete assurances that this pleasant little cottage would be anything but a temporary way station.

"Yes, of course." He put down the goblet and reached across the table so he might take my free hand in his. "I understand. And I will do everything in my power to make sure this life is not too hard for you." A pause, during which I was all too aware of the pressure of his fingers on mine, the warmth of his flesh. "And I want you to know, Marenna, that I do not expect you to do anything you do not wish to. There are two bedchambers here, and I saw how you were standing in the one and appearing to ponder the situation. I will take the smaller room, and you the larger, and when you are ready...well, you can tell me."

"Oh, I can't possibly do that to you!" I burst out. At once his eyes filled with a terrible hope, and I realized he had misunderstood me. "That is," I went on hurriedly, "you are far too tall to fit in one of those tiny beds. I will take the smaller room. You deserve your comfort, for it is only because of you and your skills that we were given this home at all."

He went very still. Slowly, he removed his hand from mine. When he spoke, his tone was still pleasant, but I thought I had come to know him somewhat, and I could hear the strain in his voice. "What kind of man would I be, to take the better room?"

"One who was acceding to my wishes," I told him. "For that is my wish...for now, anyway. I do want to be your wife, Corin. But this is all so new, and I hardly know you at all. Can you please give me the time to accept this change in my life?"

A long silence, during which I could hear the thudding of my heartbeat echoing in my ears. His face still bore that stony expression, so I could not begin to guess what he might be thinking. Or rather, I did not want to guess. I knew that many men would have said I certainly was not the first bride to have met her husband on her wedding day, and such a remark would only have been the truth. However, I had spent some time with Corin and had already seen that he was a good man, honest and considerate. All I could do was hope that he would find the forbearance to put up with me and my whims.

If not...well, I would also not be the first bride who was forced to the marriage bed, although I sincerely doubted Corin would behave in such a way.

"Very well," he said at last. "I do not wish to argue with you, and I understand your hesitancy. I can only hope that you will change your mind, given time."

"I know I will," I said stoutly. "Time is all I need, Corin...truly."

He reached for his goblet again, this time draining its contents. "I can only hope that is the way of things. For now, though, I am weary. It has been a long day, and tomorrow starts very early. I think I shall retire for the evening."

"I am sorry," I said, and did not attempt to hide the worry in my tone.

To my surprise, he smiled and got up from the table so he might come over to me. His hand touched my hair, and he bent and placed a very gentle kiss on one cheek. "There is nothing to be sorry about, my lady wife. But would you do me the favor of clearing the table, so I might go directly to bed?"

"Of course," I replied, although I had only a hazy idea as to what I should do with the leftover food. There must be a pantry, mustn't there? And a larder of some sort? Despite my inner worries, I did my best to keep my doubts from revealing themselves in my face and added, "Sleep well, Corin."

He did not answer, but only nodded and left the room. I sat there and stared at the uneaten food, and did my best not to sigh.

Even though I had been following my heart, I could not help but think that I had just made a very great mistake.

⊗⅋⊗

Corin was gone when I awoke the next morning. I did not know why this should have surprised me so much, for I was utterly weary by the time I laid my head on the pillow the night before, and I had never been in the habit of rising with the sun. Its rays were what woke me, streaming in through the thin curtains at the window, rousing me to an empty house.

In a way, that made matters easier. I could rise from my narrow bed and wash my face and hands, and get dressed in the linen gown I'd worn the day before—even though its hem was still dusty and the entire garment quite wrinkled —all without having to worry about whether Corin might interrupt me as I finished my toilette.

But the little house felt achingly empty without him. I went into the kitchen and saw that he had cut himself a slice of bread but left the cold chicken pie untouched, and had washed not just his own plate, but our dirty dishes from the night before, which I had been unable to clean, for there had been nothing to wash them with. Now a large earthen-ware jug sat at one end of the wooden counter, filled nearly to the top with water. He must have gone and gotten water from the well and brought it back here, all while I slept like the spoiled child that I was.

Well, I would have to prove to him that I could be useful, even if I had only the haziest idea of how to make myself an asset to our new household, and perhaps not as much desire to do so as I should. It still rankled that I should have to perform such chores, even though I knew that standing in the kitchen and pouting about my situation would do nothing to make it any easier.

Corin had already washed the dishes, but I found a clean cloth to finish drying them, and then set them back in the cupboard, as I did with the goblets. Putting them away made me think of the dinner my husband and I had shared the night before. It had started out so well, but by the end, he was less than pleased with me.

I could not go back and alter the words we had exchanged, so the only option I had going forward was to try to make him see it was not that I found him unappealing in any way—quite the opposite, in fact—but only that I needed time to come to terms with my new life. Once the two of us had begun to know each better, then I truly believed I could be happy with him...or at least as happy as I would ever be in such a rustic existence, deprived of all the fine things I had grown up thinking were my right.

Since we had cleaned the evening before, I did not have a great deal to do, actually. I thought of my other gown, the one I had worn as I left my father's castle, and wondered if I should attempt to launder it. The water Corin had brought did not seem as if it would be sufficient to the task, but I supposed I needed to see if there was a wash basin anywhere in the cottage. We would need one to take our baths as well, for of course this humble little dwelling did not have anything like the beautiful built-in tub of fine marble that I had once taken so much for granted.

Thinking of that bathtub, and of the luxury of having servants to heat the water and fill it, caused me to heave quite the heavy sigh. There were so many commonplaces of life that servants made so much easier! And now I would have to be the servant for both my husband and myself, for he had his own work to do, and it fell to me to become the drudge.

I realized I was teetering nearly on the brink of despair, and tears began to sting my eyes. While I knew that weeping would certainly not do me any good, it was harder than I'd thought to force those tears away. A great lump grew in my throat, and one or two of the dreadful little things began to trail their way down my cheeks. I reached up to blot them and tried to tell myself that I was being very foolish, and not at all how a daughter of the house of Sedren should be comporting herself.

This internal scolding did not have the desired effect, unfortunately. Those first few tears were followed by more, and soon enough I had a veritable river flowing down my face. What made the situation even worse was that I did not have a handkerchief, for I had not thought to bring any with me. I supposed I could look in Corin's pack to see if he had any cloths I could use, but that seemed like a terrible intrusion. He certainly had not given me leave to paw through his things.

After a moment, I realized I could use the dishcloth, which I had left hanging from a hook in the kitchen so it might dry. I left the main room and went in search of the dishcloth, and then used it to blot my eyes as best I could. At least the cloth was already damp, and so if Corin came home now for any reason, he wouldn't think it strange that the fabric wasn't dry.

Of course, that didn't help me with what I was sure must be a pair of reddened eyes. The cottage didn't have a mirror—they were far too costly—but I guessed that I must look quite the fright. I went back into the room where I had slept and made up the bed, since that would give me something to do. While the result was somewhat lumpy, and nothing like the smooth perfection my old bed used to be when the maids were finished with it, at least it was a task I could manage on my own. When I was done, I stood at the window and looked out at the bright morning, forcing myself to breathe calmly and to let the sunlight touch my face, warm, reassuring.

Doing so did help me to calm down somewhat. Once I was sure that I wouldn't dissolve into another bout of tears, I went into Corin's room, thinking I could make his bed as well. Of course he had already taken care of that particular chore—and much more neatly than I had with my own narrow bed. Who knew that making up a bed required such particular skills?

Although I knew I should leave, go back to the kitchen and look for a wash basin, something compelled me to go to the wardrobe and open its door. Inside hung several heavy linen shirts similar to the one Corin had worn the day before, and a linen vest and doublet, both looking rather wrinkled. He must have had them in his pack, choosing to wear the sturdier suede weskit as he traveled.

I reached out and touched the sleeve of one of the shirts, feeling the slight roughness of the fabric under my fingertips. In that moment, I experienced such a wave of longing, I almost began to weep again. How foolish I had been! For I was Corin's wife, and I should not have denied him. Exactly what I was denying him, I still did not precisely know, but this was certainly not a normal state of affairs. The night before I had pleaded for more time, true, and yet now I did not know precisely what I was waiting for. It was not as if I could go back to the life I had before. I must embrace the future, and that future meant Corin.

A very fine sentiment, and one easy enough to form while I was here alone. Whether I would be able to hold on to that resolve when he was once again in my presence, I had no idea. Indeed, I did not even know whether he would come home to have his luncheon, or whether he would take it in the field with the rest of the workers.

Someone knocked at the door then, and I startled. Who on earth could be coming to visit me here?

Perhaps it is someone with your allotment of food, I told myself. *Master Brinsell did say that someone would be by with that today.*

This seemed the most reasonable explanation for a visitor, although I was not precisely cheered at the thought of a food delivery the way some people might be. Once I had accepted the food and brought it into my kitchen, that meant I must do something with it.

Still, it would be the height of rudeness to leave whoever was at the door waiting there indefinitely while I dithered. I closed the wardrobe and hurried to the front door, then quickly opened it.

Standing outside was a young woman probably a few years older than myself, with an enormous basket dangling from one arm. She was taller than I, dark-haired like most Sirlendians, but with unusual hazel-green eyes. I would not say she was precisely pretty, for her nose was too long and her mouth somewhat wide, but perhaps most observers would be so mesmerized by her eyes that they would not pay attention to the rest of her features.

She smiled at me, showing off uneven but very white teeth. "Are you Marenna Blackstone?"

I was tempted to ask who else she thought I might be, but realized that would be a foolish way to begin our acquaintance. This young woman might end up being an ally, or even a friend.

I thought I could use a friend in this place.

Smiling, I replied, "Yes, I am. Please, come in."

She came into the cottage's main room and gave a frankly appraising look around. "I hadn't thought you would be able to get it cleaned up so quickly."

"Oh, it was mostly dust and cobwebs." I thought it better not to mention that my husband had done the bulk of the work, since I could not be sure whether such a revelation would make her think less of me. "And you are...?"

Another flash of a smile. "I am Lynnis

Oakfell. My husband has worked the land here for ten years."

Lynnis certainly didn't look old enough to me to have been married for ten years, unless she had come here as a child bride. But quite possibly they had wed after her husband had already been employed at the estate for some time.

"It is very nice to meet you, Mistress Oakfell. Please, let me take that basket from you."

This time I was the one on the receiving end of the appraising glance, rather than the house. "It is quite heavy. Why don't you let me take it into the kitchen?"

I didn't argue; she knew far better than I how much that basket must weigh. "That's very kind of you. Please, come this way."

She followed me into the kitchen and set the basket down on the counter. Once again she glanced around, those lively hazel eyes taking in every detail. I sent a silent thank-you to the gods that I had taken the time to finish tidying up in here, for I doubted she could find much that was amiss.

"So your husband is the new under-overseer?"

"For now," I said. "I suppose we shall have to

see what happens when the former under-over-seer recovers from his injury."

"Master Threnson," Lynnis supplied. "He never cared all that much for the work, to be honest. My husband and I both think he broke his leg on purpose."

"Oh, that cannot be true," I protested, even though her words kindled new hope within me. If this Master Threnson truly had no taste for his work with the vines, then perhaps Corin had a true chance of being able to keep his position permanently.

She grinned. "Oh, it most certainly is. And Hal and I also think Master Threnson is hoping that his Grace will compensate him handsomely for his injury, enough so he will be able to go off and make his fortune in the city." A slight wrinkling of her nose told me how much she thought of this scheme.

"You do not care for cities?"

"Oh, no," she replied at once. "Hal took me to Iselfex once, told me I must see it, as it's said to be one of the wonders of the world. Well, the buildings are very fine —at least in the districts where the nobles have their town houses—but gods, all those people packed together! Combined with the stink off the river in the heat of the summer, the smell of it nearly knocked me down. I was glad to come back here to Marric's Rest and breathe good country air, that is for certain. And I have no desire to leave ever again."

Since I hadn't been to the capital since I was a little girl, I couldn't comment on her observations of the place. Certainly I did not remember it being so foul, but then, we had visited in the autumn, when it was cooler, and besides, we had not gone about in the poorer sections of the city.

"Were you born here on the estate?" I inquired.

"Yes, as was Hal. We grew up together, and so it made sense for us to marry."

I supposed it would. If I had had a friend who was a boy, who had been my partner in childhood games, would I have also wished for him to be my partner in life once I was grown?

Perhaps. It didn't really matter, however, for of course there had not been anyone like that for me. "And Lord Sorthannic is a good master?"

I had taken care to keep my tone as neutral as possible while I asked the question, but all the same, Lynnis lifted an eyebrow at me, as though she guessed there was some subtext to the inquiry beyond simple curiosity. "Oh, yes," she replied. "Now, of course he didn't grow up here, but came to us from South Eredor, where his father lived in exile. But after his Grace had finished his sword training with Duke Senric, he came here to take over the estate. He's done very well, even if he wasn't raised to it from the beginning, so to speak."

The story wasn't completely unfamiliar to me, although I was forced to admit that I had not paid as much attention to Lord Sorthannic's unorthodox past as perhaps I might. "His mother was a commoner, I believe?"

Once again, Lynnis arched her eyebrow, even as I belatedly realized that someone married to a farm worker most likely did not often employ the term "commoner." To my relief, however, she appeared to let it go, saying, "Yes. Her family was prosperous, though, from what I've heard, had owned vineyards in South Eredor for generations. That was why Lord Sorthannic was so eager to try growing his own grapes here—he already knew a great deal about the process and thought he should be successful."

"And so he is."

Although I had not phrased the words as a question, Lynnis seemed to take them as such. "Very much so. The vines are young compared to some in the south, but they've done well. Our wines are much in demand in the capital. Not that his Grace has need of the money, because of course he inherited such a fine estate, but it helps all the rest of us. He pays the workers well, gives us a place to live and food for our table." Her gaze moved to the basket sitting on the counter. "Perhaps I should help you with that."

"Oh, it's not necessary—" I began, but she waved a hand.

"It's my pleasure. I already have today's chores managed at my own cottage, and with Hal off in the fields and not due to come back until sundown, I might as well do something to amuse myself."

"So the workers don't come home for their luncheon?"

"No. But," she added quickly, perhaps wanting to make sure I knew this was no real hardship, "the kitchens in the castle always send down a fine spread for them, so I daresay they fare better than we do. But let us get all this put away."

Before I could stop her, she began emptying the basket, bringing out all manner of foodstuffs —potatoes and carrots and fine red apples, and a small bag of flour, a jar of honey, and so much more that I began to wonder if a spell had been placed on the basket so its inside was larger than its outside. Not that anyone in Sirlende would dare to work such a spell, for magic was strictly forbidden here. Even so....

With a brisk economy of movement that told me she had a great deal of practice in such things, Lynnis put all the food away in the cupboards, and the small squishy packet she said was a good cut of meat for stew in the cold larder, so it might not spoil. Of course, I hadn't the faintest idea how to make stew, although I thought that perhaps the meat should go in a pot with the potatoes and carrots...after they had all been cut into small pieces.

"You seem rather lost, Marenna," Lynnis remarked as she turned back to me.

"Oh, I am just unfamiliar with this kitchen and perhaps still wearied from my journey yesterday."

Although these explanations sounded perfectly rational to me, it seemed that my companion wasn't quite convinced. "Have you ever made stew?"

"Well...." It was on the tip of my tongue to hand her an easy lie, but if she asked any further questions, she would at once know the depths of my prevarication. "No," I said miserably.

Surprise flashed in her big hazel eyes, but she only said, "Do you know how to cook *anything?*"

Mutely, I shook my head.

To my consternation, Lynnis chuckled. "Oh,

your husband has quite a bargain in you, hasn't he? It's a good thing you're so beautiful."

Since she had tempered her insult with a compliment, I did not know how I should respond. My first instinct had been to say that of course I had never learned to cook, because I had always had servants to take on those tasks for me. However, Corin and I had agreed during our journey here that we would not speak of my origins, so I knew I would have to give Lynnis a different story.

"I—I was raised by a stepmother," I lied, remembering my promise to come up with a sensible explanation for my lack of domestic skills. "She did not care for me, and went out of her way to make sure I knew as little about being a good wife as possible. I was forbidden to set foot in the kitchen, and so I never learnt how to cook. The only reason I am handy with my needle is that I was able to spy on her as she sewed by the fireplace at night, and perhaps had a natural aptitude for the work, but I fear that I am not, as you said, much of a 'bargain' when it comes to anything else."

"Oh, well," Lynnis said, her tone brisk, as if she did not wish for me to burden her with my tale of woe. "That is too bad, but perhaps we can strike something of a bargain. I am a very good cook, but I have never been good at the needle arts. If I teach you how to cook, will you school me in the mysterious art of sewing? I know that Hal would be forever grateful to have darns in his socks that don't look like great blobs, or patches on his trousers that inevitably begin to come loose after only a few weeks."

"That would be wonderful," I replied, overflowing with gratitude…and relief. "Sewing is not so very difficult, after all."

"For you, perhaps." She held out her hand. "Shall we shake on it and seal the bargain?"

I did not even stop to think. I took her hand and shook it heartily. Perhaps I would not have to worry about poisoning Corin with my cooking after all.

"Now then," Lynnis said, a twinkle in her eyes seeming to tell me that she had guessed at my thoughts. "Let us put together a proper meal for that handsome husband of yours."

CHAPTER 7

I<small>T WAS NEARLY DARK WHEN</small> C<small>ORIN FINALLY CAME</small> home, his clothing stained with the juice of the grape clusters he had spent the day picking. Only that morning, I would have been dismayed by the sight of those stains, worrying as to how I would ever manage to get his garments clean again. But Lynnis had promised to help me with the laundry on the morrow, and I had no doubt that my capable new friend would have everything right as rain.

Corin paused in the middle of the cottage's main room and lifted his head to take an appreciative sniff at the air. The stew had been gently simmering over the fire nearly all day, and Lynnis had also helped me to bake a small loaf of bread, whose warm aroma joined with that of the stew to make a particularly toothsome smell.

"Is that...?" he began, then stopped. Perhaps he feared if he asked a direct question about dinner, he would get an answer he did not like.

"It is your dinner, my husband," I said. "Beef stew and fresh bread. And there are apples and honey for dessert, if you have need of more than the stew and the bread."

Startled disbelief was clear on his features, but he merely smiled at me. "Well, then, such a splendid repast deserves a clean shirt. Let me go and change, Marenna, and then we will sit down to supper together."

"I'll get the food on the table," I promised.

He smiled again, and left the room. I had already set the table with plates and bowls and cutlery, and clean linens to wipe our hands, so all that was left was to bring out the pot of stew and set it on a trivet, thus protecting the surface of the table. Oh, and the bread, of course—once the stew was safely deposited, I went back to fetch the fresh loaf and some butter, and brought it to the table as well.

By the time I was done with those tasks, Corin had reappeared, wearing a clean shirt and with his hair neatly brushed and tied back. He eyed the table with approval, then said, "It all looks very well, except it is missing one thing."

"What is that?" I asked, surveying the tabletop and the various items arrayed upon it. As far as I could tell, I had not forgotten anything.

"Stew which smells as good as that deserves a good bottle of wine to go with it," he replied. "Let me fetch some from the cupboard."

"I can get it—"

"No, I shall. You have already worked very hard this afternoon, I can see."

Guilt bubbled up in me then, for of course it was Lynnis who had done most of the work. Yes, she had made me assist her, and had carefully supervised my cutting of the meat and carrots and onions and potatoes, but still, the whole thing would have been an inedible mess if it had not been for her guidance. I had thought to put out a bottle of wine, but had decided against it, believing such things should be saved for special occasions. But perhaps Lord Sorthannic was as generous with his wine as he seemed to be in all other things, and we would not have to worry about rationing ourselves.

Corin emerged from the kitchen with a bottle and two more stoneware goblets, for I had already set the table with a pair of them and filled them with water. Using the short dagger he wore at his hip, he pried out the cork from the bottle and poured a good measure of wine into each of the glasses.

"To my beautiful wife, and to the meal she has prepared for us," he said, lifting a goblet.

I clanked mine against his, glad to see that his dark mood of the night before appeared to have lifted. Perhaps it was nothing more than relief that at least I would not starve him, but he did seem quite cheerful, especially for someone who had spent his entire day hard at work in the fields.

"How was your day, Corin?"

He smiled. No, rather, he beamed, as if he had drunk in the bright sunshine all day and now had no choice but to reflect it outward. "Excellent," he replied. "The vineyards are beautiful, and managed very well. Master Brinsell definitely knows what he is doing. And ah, the grapes we harvested today were also beautiful. I think this is going to be a superior vintage, once the wine we make this autumn is ready to be drunk."

"That's wonderful to hear. But is it not very hard work?"

"Perhaps," Corin said with a shrug. "But it is good, honest work. And the beauty of a grape harvest lies in thinking of what all those lovely clusters will become, how in a few years' time, we will have wonderful wine. Yes, perhaps it does not satisfy the stomach like a potato or a carrot"—he gestured with his free hand toward the pot of stew where it sat on its trivet—"but there is something about wine that enriches the soul."

I had never heard him speak in such a way before, and my heart warmed toward him that much more. Yes, we were still almost strangers to one another, but already I judged him to be a good man. What whim had driven him to accept my father's mad proposal, I still did not know, although I was almost certain now that it was not because he desired a woman he could control, or abuse.

"It is lovely," I agreed. "And I suppose you appreciate it all the more because you know so intimately what is required to make it." I sipped some of my wine, then nodded. "Perhaps I will never have quite as detailed knowledge as yours, but I hope to learn from you, so I might share in that appreciation."

"That is something I have always hoped for— that I might someday have a partner to share in this part of my life." He smiled at me, then picked up his spoon and gathered up a mouthful of stew.

His expression changed to one of wonder as he chewed, and he tilted his head at me, clearly surprised. "This is most excellent, Marenna. I did not know you had any experience in the kitchen."

Of course I did not. That the stew was at all tasty—and it was, despite not being anything near as fancy as the stuffed quail my father so loved, or the lamb ragout which had lately been a favorite of mine in the springtime—was due entirely to Lynnis' efforts. I knew I should tell Corin the truth, that the most I had done was chop a few vegetables and keep an eye on the stew as it cooked so it would simmer gently rather than boil.

And yet, when I opened my mouth to let him know that I had only been an assistant in the kitchen and nothing more, I found I could not reveal the truth. I wanted him to believe that I had made our dinner, that I was not quite the useless noblewoman he clearly thought me. Besides, it was such a harmless little lie...barely that, even. A sin of omission and nothing more.

"Oh, it was not so very difficult," I lied. "I cut up the meat and the vegetables, and used some of the wine and spices I had on hand to make the base. After that, it was mostly keeping watch over it and adjusting things from time to time. When I was younger, I did like to visit the kitchens and see what was being made, and how it was done. I learned a good deal simply from watching."

"Yes, that much is apparent." Corin spooned up some more of the stew, ate it, and gave an approving nod. "And here I had been worrying about how you would manage in the kitchen."

"Well, you have no need to worry, because everything should go just fine." Then, thinking I was being a bit too sure of myself, I added quickly, "That is, as long as I am preparing simple dishes. I rather doubt I could put together a feast like my father used to have at Midwinter, but if I am cooking for only the two of us, we should do well enough."

A faint shadow passed over his face at the phrase "only the two of us," but he merely nodded and broke off a piece of bread, then spread it thickly with butter. "I certainly would not expect a roast suckling pig, or a dish I heard of that was served at the imperial palace—roast peacock with its feathers all reattached, so at first people were not sure whether it was alive or not."

I repressed a shudder at that image. True, I had heard of such extravagances, and had seen dishes nearly as outlandish at feasts hosted by some of our neighboring nobles, but my father had never participated in such displays. Our household could have afforded it, I supposed; however, despite the wealth our silver mines had brought to us, he preferred for his household to live more modestly.

"I would think those peacock feathers would be put to better use in a lady's fan," I remarked as I took some bread for myself and bit into it. Yes, Lynnis had a deft hand at baking as well, for the loaf was fine and light and yet somehow rich at the same time.

"And without having to kill the peacock," Corin said. "Which I'm sure would meet with the peacock's approval as well, although I have to admit that they are nasty, disagreeable birds."

"Are they? We never kept any. I know it is the fashion, but my father could never stand the cries they make."

"There was a flock on one of the estates where I worked. The peacocks did seem to enjoy chasing humans—one time, they pursued one of the fellows who worked in the fields, and he took off in such a panic that he bolted right up and over a fence to get away from them. Unfortunately, that fence enclosed the pigpen, so you can imagine what a state he was in by the time he extricated himself."

I giggled. No, I had never spent much time around pigs, but even I knew how much their pens could stink, and I could imagine how difficult it must be to get rid of that smell, once it had penetrated someone's clothing and hair. "Then I will be glad that we have no peacocks here in this little hamlet, for I am not sure I could get away from one of them quickly enough, should it take it into its head to come chasing after me." I drank some wine to wash down the bread I had just eaten, then inquired, "Does Lord Sorthannic have any peacocks up at the castle?"

Corin had been smiling as he recounted his story, but his expression went rather blank as he shook his head. "As to that, I am not sure, for of course we field hands are not invited to enter his Grace's home."

"'Field hand'?" I echoed. "I thought you were the under-overseer."

A small shrug, and he also reached for his goblet of wine. "As to that, right now I am mainly another strong back and a quick pair of hands. My experience will come more to bear once it is time to crush the grapes and move them into their vats."

"Ah." I hadn't thought of the situation in those terms, but I supposed it made sense that right now the most important thing was to get the fruit off the vines and safely away from any predatory birds or insects. Given the lovely mild weather we'd been enjoying, an early frost wasn't terribly likely, although I knew it had happened before and no doubt would happen again. "How many days of picking do you have to go?"

"Probably another three or four. This was a good year, with a large yield. And there are not so many of us—ten in all, because of course not everyone can work on the same crop. Master Brinsell also has workers bringing in the wheat, and the beans, and so many other things. The kitchen gardens are mostly supervised by the staff at the castle, so the rest of us can focus on the larger crops."

So much to keep track of. I supposed I hadn't given much thought to where the food on my table back home in Silverhold had come from, because of course my father had his own overseers to manage everything. I did remember the castle's extensive kitchen gardens, though, for as a child I had loved to slip out and steal the slipper beans and eat them, warm and fresh, straight from their vines. "And after that?"

Corin's dark eyes met mine, and I had to force myself not to look away. His gaze offered a promise of something I did not entirely understand, although I knew it must include the two of us working through it together. "After that...we shall have to see. However, judging by a few of the comments made by the other workers today, it sounds as though my predecessor had no great stomach for this sort of work, which means I am...hopeful."

Since Lynnis had said much the same thing, I thought our prospects for remaining here did seem much more promising than they had the day before. However, since I had not yet made any mention of my newfound friend, I decided to keep my observation to myself, saying only, "Well, that does seem to bode well, does it not? And once you are done with the harvest and have gone on to actually begin making the wine, you can show them how much of an expert you are. I have no doubt that Master Brinsell will be very pleased."

The corners of Corin's mouth lifted. Clearly, he was happy to hear my praise, even if he himself was still not quite sure of what the future might hold. "I suppose we will just have to wait and see. For now, though, let us enjoy this wonderful dinner you have made."

Guilt over the lie I had told—or rather, the truth I had not told—made me want to squirm in my chair, but I forced myself smile at my husband and nod in agreement.

After all, I had plenty of time to let him know

exactly how I had become so proficient in the kitchen.

⚜

The next morning, I was not so tired that I did not hear Corin leave his room and go into the kitchen to get himself a small bite to eat— perhaps a piece of the leftover bread, and some tea. I lay awake, staring at the ceiling, and wondered whether I should get up and spend that time with him. Wasn't that something husbands and wives were supposed to do together? I had to confess that I truly did not know, for of course my mother had passed away when I was only an infant, and my father had never remarried. My only examples of marriage were those of our neighbors, and, to a lesser extent, my own brothers. Even so, I had never seen them interact with their wives in anything except formal social settings, and therefore had little idea as to how they behaved when they were alone together.

My cowardice made the decision for me, because after I had lain there in bed for a few minutes, I heard the front door to the cottage close and knew I was alone again. I supposed I should be relieved that Corin did not wish to disturb me, wanted me to get as much sleep as possible, but at the same time, I felt somewhat abandoned, as though he should have cared enough about sharing my company that he would wake me so he might start his day with me in his presence.

I tried to tell myself that I could not have it both ways. Either I wanted to hold him at arm's length as I had so far, or I wanted more than that, even if I still was not precisely sure what that "more" might mean.

Excruciating as the prospect was, I knew I must take a bath that day. Never in my life had I gone so long without bathing, and even though I knew the task would be a joyless one, neither did I want to spend another day without clean hair or a clean body.

And yes, the endeavor took me more than an hour, an hour during which I had to heat pot after pot of hot water over the kitchen fire, and then dump it into the large wooden tub I would use later that day to do the laundry. As it was, because it required so much time to get a pot of water hot, by the time it was ready to be dumped into the tub, the water I had previously heated was already lukewarm. Still, it was not cold, and between the heat from the fireplace and the warmth of my own exertions, I did not take any kind of chill. My mind recoiled at the thought of what such an endeavor would be like in the depths of winter, and I put that unpleasant reality away to think about later.

Although I only had the two everyday gowns, one of which I would be washing later, Sendra had packed an entire week's worth of chemises and underthings for me, so at least all the garments that touched my skin were clean, even if the dress was not. I sat by the fire and combed out my damp hair, then worked it into a long braid, which I wrapped up with the same silken cord my maid had used to bind my hair when I left the castle. As my fingers wrestled with my half-dry tresses, I wondered what Sendra was doing right now. Had she already left the castle to join my brother Evander's household, or had my father allowed her to stay on for a while longer, so she might dispose of my wardrobe and properly close up the elegant suite of rooms that had once been mine?

The thought of all my gowns given away to my sisters-in-law, or perhaps to other members of the household, quite distressed me, and the image that formed in my mind, of all the furnishings in my rooms covered with green baize, or worse, sent to languish in the castle's cellars with the rest of the family's cast-offs, was even worse.

Although I tried to tell myself I had nothing to weep about—after all, my dinner with Corin the evening before had been most pleasant—I felt a tear slip from the corner of my eye and trail its way down my nose, followed by another, then another. And—

"Oh, my," came Lynnis' voice. She stood at the kitchen door and peered in at me, worry clear on her features. "Whatever is the matter?"

Had she knocked? I couldn't recall her knocking on the door, but then, I had been so lost in my thoughts, it was distinctly possible that I simply hadn't heard her.

"Oh, it is nothing," I replied, reaching up to blot away my tears.

She came into the kitchen and set the small pail she'd been carrying down on the countertop so she might plant her hands on her hips. "That certainly didn't look like nothing. Have you and your husband quarreled?"

"No, not at all," I said. At least that was the truth. "We had a most pleasant dinner last night, and he was very happy with everything he ate. I suppose I was only feeling a bit melancholy and homesick, even though I really don't have much that I miss there. I will be fine."

"Well, that is good to hear." Lynnis paused there and I tensed, worried that she might ask

whether I had told Corin who was really responsible for our dinner of the evening before.
Instead, she cast an amused eye at my still-damp
hair and went on, "I hope you are not so wearied
from your bath this morning that you don't wish
to do laundry."

"Oh, no," I replied stoutly. "My other gown is
in quite a state, as is the shirt Corin wore in the
fields yesterday. I need to learn how to take care
of such things."

She smiled. "It is not so very difficult. But first
—more hot water."

And the tedium of it began all over again.
Since I had used up all the water Corin had
brought in earlier, Lynnis and I had to go to the
well, where we met some of the other women
from our little settlement—Caislyn, and Terlissa,
and so many others. They were curious about
me, but they seemed to accept Lynnis' explanation that she was showing me the well and the
other points of interest in the hamlet, and didn't
appear eager to inquire further. Well, they most
likely had their own chores to attend to, and did
not want to waste time with idle questions.

Lynnis and I lugged our containers of water
back to the kitchen and poured them into the pot
on the fire so the water might begin to heat up. I
went and fetched the garments that needed to be

washed. Lynnis inspected them with a critical eye and said there was nothing so very wrong with my gown except some dust on the hem. But Corin's shirt she dampened in advance, and got a thick yellow bar of soap out of the pail she'd brought, along with a stiff-bristled brush, and rubbed the soap on the worst of the stains before setting the shirt aside so the soap might do its work.

"There are a dozen families that live here," she said as we waited for the water to boil. "More of the workers live in Elmcroft, but it's better to be here on the estate, for then the men do not have to travel so far to begin their work in the fields each day."

"'Families,'" I echoed. Yes, I had heard the cries and laughter of children the day before, but I realized that Lynnis had made no mention of any children of her own. Certainly she was not old enough to have sons who could work in the fields. "And your children?"

For the first time since I'd met her, she looked rather uncomfortable. But then she lifted her shoulders and smiled at me, although something about her expression seemed rather forced. "Oh, Hal and I have none yet...although it is certainly not for lack of trying!"

"'Trying'?" I repeated, not sure what she

meant. That there was some mysterious process that resulted in children, I was aware, but the details had so far eluded me.

Her eyebrows lifted. "Well, you know."

I shook my head. "No, I am afraid I don't."

A long pause during which she stared at me, as if she was attempting to discover whether I was playing some kind of jest on her. Then she said, "You mean that you and your husband have not...?"

"Have not what?"

"Oh, gods," she said, after expelling a breath of consternation. "You truly meant it when you said that your stepmother had not told you anything of how to be a good wife."

"Yes," I replied. I had not liked telling Lynnis such a lie, but it seemed it was serving me in good stead now, if it meant I could continue to blame that mythical stepmother for any of my numerous shortcomings in the domestic arena.

"Your Corin must be a very patient man."

"I—" Whatever defense I might have tried to summon then fled, because I knew that she was right. He *had* been very patient with me, although I still hadn't quite discovered the reasoning behind such patience.

"Were you never around any livestock? Did you never see them in the springtime, when their blood ran hot and they wanted to mate and have lambs and calves and so forth?"

"No," I said simply. It was only the truth. Of course I knew that animals had babies, just as people had babies, but I had never learnt anything of the mysterious process that made them appear in the first place. And while we had plenty of animals on the estate, I had never spent very much time around them. Perhaps I could be forgiven for such an omission, because when I was a young child, I had become quite enamored of the little lambs...only to be terribly distressed when I discovered that they were to end up on our dinner table. I had not eaten lamb for years after that.

"Oh...dear." I did not know Lynnis very well yet, but already I had gathered the impression that she was someone who was not frequently at a loss for words. She got up from where she had been sitting and went to pour some of the water from the pot into the tub, then dumped all the clothing to be washed—Corin's shirts and my chemises and my one other serviceable gown, along with the stained shirt we'd already scrubbed with soap—into that tub so it might soak. While these were tasks that needed to be done, I rather thought she had busied herself in such a fashion so she could avoid answering me right away.

"I suppose you must think I am very foolish," I said.

"No," she replied at once. "Sheltered, yes. But I do not think you are a fool, Marenna. Come here now, so you can get to work on these clothes. Like this."

She showed me how to rub the soap on the stains, and scrub at them with the hard-bristled brush. The combination did work quite well, and seemed a much simpler thing than putting a meal together, although I could not help but inwardly fret over what the hot water and the rough soap would do to my hands. I worked in silence for a few minutes while she watched me with a careful eye. However, it seemed that not all her attention was focused on making sure I did not harm the garments, or miss a spot, because at length she spoke, her voice careful, considering.

"I can see that your husband is being gentle with you, because it seems he must understand that you have come to him without truly knowing what your duties are as his wife. And you are very newly married."

"Only two days," I pointed out, after double-checking that I truly had gotten that one terrible blotch off the cuff of Corin's shirt. I wrung it out and draped it over the edge of the tub, and went on to one of my chemises, which really didn't require much attention.

"Yes." She hesitated, then went on, "So it has not been long enough for him to become angry, or impatient. However, you can't expect matters to continue in such a way forever." Another pause, during which she fixed me with a keen eye. "Nor should you want them to, not when you are married to such a handsome man. Tell me, has he even kissed you?"

"During the ceremony," I said, suddenly shy. I was not sure why I should feel so reticent, but a blush stole over my cheeks and I looked away from her, intent on scrubbing at a stain that was not there. "And once the next day...but only on my cheek."

"Oh." After that response, she got up from the chair where she'd been sitting and came over to the tub, then lifted Corin's shirt and looked it over carefully. I must have done a respectable job, because she nodded and laid it aside. "Well, kissing is usually where it starts. But believe me, there is far more to what transpires between a man and his wife than merely a kiss."

I tried to imagine more than a kiss. Corin had kissed me on the lips and on the cheek, but what if he kissed me somewhere else, such as the back of my neck, or the inside of my wrist. Or....

The thought came to me of precisely where he might bestow a kiss, and blood flooded my cheeks once again.

"I see that you're beginning to understand," Lynnis said with a grin. "But, just so you are entirely clear...."

And from there she went on to explain, in simple but very detailed terms, exactly what was expected of the marriage bed. I stared at her, gape-mouthed, and tried to imagine Corin and myself participating in that kind of activity.

Of course I failed utterly.

"So...that is how you get with child?"

"Yes. Now you see why I said that it wasn't because of lack of trying that we did not yet have any children."

"And you...enjoy it?"

"Of course I do!" she said with a laugh. "It is one of the most wonderful things in the world. Only," she went on, her expression sobering somewhat, "it can hurt a bit the first time. After that, though, all should be well."

I contemplated that piece of information for a moment. "And how did you learn all this?"

"Why, from my mother, of course. The day after Hal asked my parents for permission to marry me, my mother sat me down and explained all that would be expected of me once I was his wife."

"Oh." Many times over the years I had mourned my mother's loss, had wondered what it would have been like to have her with me to offer advice and comfort, and to guide me from childhood to womanhood. It would have been so very different. For one thing, I would not have been so ignorant of such obvious facts of life when I agreed to this marriage.

"I am sorry," Lynnis said. She had been watching me, and perhaps some of my sorrow had shown itself on my face. "It must have been difficult, to not have your mother with you, and to have only a cruel stepmother who did her best to make sure you were not ready to be someone's wife."

Once again I hated myself for the lie I had told her. Although I had never had a true friend, I could see that Lynnis might be one, if I would but let her. Unfortunately, I feared that once she knew the truth, she would never want to speak to me again.

"Perhaps," I allowed. I did not dare say anything more than that. "But you have helped me tremendously, Lynnis. Thank you."

"It is nothing." She went over to the counter

and retrieved the jug we used to fetch water, and said, "Let us go to the well again. We will rinse these clothes, and hang them to dry, and when your husband comes home...." A pause, and she added, again with that dancing light in her hazel eyes, "Perhaps then you will show him what a good wife you can be."

CHAPTER 8

THE CLEAN CLOTHES BOBBED ON THE CLOTHESLINE outside the kitchen window, and the cottage was filled with the scent of roasting chicken. I had dusted again, since I found a few cobwebs Corin and I had missed that first night, and the little house practically shone.

I wanted to be a proper wife to him. If only I was not so afraid.

Lynnis' revelations had not made me feel better about the situation...rather the reverse. Because now the mystery had been explained to me, and although my friend had sworn that the marriage bed was a wonderful thing, I was not sure I believed her. Taken purely on a physical and factual level, the act did seem more than a little frightening.

Besides, she had known Hal well when they were married—they had grown up in the hamlet here together, were childhood friends before they were sweethearts. She would have been relaxed and easy with him, whereas I did not see how I could possibly be relaxed when expected to engage in such activities with a person I hardly knew.

But perhaps...perhaps I should allow Corin to kiss me more. Yes, that seemed like a good, cautious first step. After all, I had enjoyed that first kiss, even while I had writhed at the thought of having to marry a perfect stranger. Once I was comfortable with kissing him, then perhaps it would not be so difficult to allow matters to progress further.

The door opened and he entered, just as windblown and grape-stained as he had been the day before. But he smiled at me and said, "I see that you have had yet another productive day."

"I hope so, Corin." Inwardly, I winced at the sight of his filthy shirt, for it brought home to me the realization that all these chores would be never-ending, that as soon as I was done with one, I would have at least three more tasks to manage. However, I tried to push the thought away, because I truly was happy to see the way he smiled at me. I let my gaze linger on his lips, and wondered what it would be like to have him kiss me again—*truly* kiss me, sweep me into his arms and hold me close, rather than have such a chaste embrace as the one we'd shared during our wedding ceremony.

Something in the air between us seemed to change then, and his gaze fastened on mine and held. My heart began to beat harder in my chest, and I realized my knees felt somewhat weak.

"I—I need to look in on our dinner," I managed, and hurried away before he could say anything to stop me.

Nor did he attempt any kind of pursuit. I heard his footsteps go down the hall, where he no doubt was headed toward his room so he might change his shirt. After checking on the chicken and assuring myself that it was cooking evenly, I took up a basket, went outside, and began pulling down our clothes from the line I had strung between two trees. The shirts and chemises were now dry and smelled sweet from hanging in the hay-scented air all afternoon, and I did as Lynnis had instructed, folding the garments as I placed them in the basket so they would not get wrinkled. True, my folds were not quite as neat as the examples she had shown me, but I told myself that they should do well enough —especially Corin's shirts, since they would only get dirty again as soon as he wore them in the fields.

When I entered the kitchen, I saw him standing there, sniffing at the chicken, and casting an approving eye at the cold bean salad, which was already prepared and sitting in a bowl on the countertop.

"Dinner should be ready soon," I said, the words coming out quickly, almost tripping over themselves. I did not want another awkward silence like the one we had just shared, fraught with emotions I was not sure I could even identify. "And we will have the rest of the bread from last night."

"Once again I must express my surprise and gratitude."

Was he poking fun at me? His expression was serious enough, but a certain glint in his dark eyes seemed to indicate that he might be teasing me...just a little. "Oh, I know you had feared you would be forced to subsist on cold porridge and stale bread," I returned with a grin.

"Nothing so dire as that, I assure you." He went to the cupboard where the wine was stored and extracted another bottle. Looking past him to the shelf, I could see that only four bottles were left. Would he get more once another week began, or would we be left without once we had drunk everything we'd started with? I couldn't know for sure, and I decided it was better not to protest, even though I worried what drinking that bottle might mean, what with this strange new energy crackling between us.

Or perhaps it had always been there, and I was only now recognizing it for what it was. I might have had an easier time of it if I had had even a childhood crush on one of the young men of my acquaintance, but none of them had interested me enough to even think about stealing a kiss. I had been content to admire some of my brothers' friends from afar, since they had seemed so much older and worldlier than I. Being confronted with someone like Corin, so handsome and dedicated and passionate, made me realize everything I had been missing.

He took the bottle and a pair of goblets out to the table, and I busied myself with removing the chicken from its spit and placing it on a platter. Truly, we had been lucky in how well-supplied this cottage was; we'd only to move in, and practically everything we needed had been provided for us.

The candles on the table were flickering as I came to set down the platter with the chicken. I excused myself to get the bowl of bean salad and the little wooden board with the bread and butter, then took a seat. Corin was already sitting down; I could see how he had brushed his hair and changed his shirt, and looked perfectly respectable.

Well, perhaps not quite. A perfectly respectable man might not have had that glint in his dark eyes, one that sent another rush of warmth through me. It seemed he liked what he saw when he gazed upon me, and the feeling was more than mutual.

"Another productive day?" I inquired as he began to carve the chicken.

"Very. We have picked all the *larsonne* grapes, and have moved on to the *chersoni*. That one makes up the bulk of the harvest, so I do think we will be done in a few more days." He smiled, adding, "Once all the grapes are gathered in, we will have the crush. Of course you're invited to participate."

"'The crush'?" I repeated, uncertain of the term. "What is that?"

"The grapes must be crushed to release their juices before they go to the vats. It's the custom to have the women of the estate perform the task, for their feet are more delicate and less likely to bruise the fruit."

For a second I stared at him, not sure what on earth he meant by mentioning women's feet.

Then comprehension began to dawn. "You mean...they want us to step on the grapes?"

"More or less. It's a tradition. But since you are new to the estate, I could probably come up with some way to have you beg off."

While I didn't particularly relish the idea of smashing grapes to a pulp with my bare feet—just the thought of what such an activity would do to the hem of my chemise made me want to shudder—I knew I should be doing everything I could to fit in with the community here. If that included stomping on grapes, then so be it. "All the women do this?"

"Well, most of them," Corin replied. He sipped some of his wine, and added, "Some of the more elderly women cannot manage it anymore because of the pain in their joints, but everyone else joins in."

Which meant that Lynnis would be among those participating in the crush. I thought I could manage to perform a task I otherwise would view as completely undignified, as long as I had my friend with me. "Then I shall join in as well," I said. "I do not want to be seen as someone who sits by while others work."

The look Corin sent me then was fond, almost as caressing as a touch on my cheek or hair. I wanted to bask in that gaze...but I also realized I wanted him to touch me. We had been so formal with one another, which was mostly my fault. I would have to determine the best way to fix that situation. "I doubt anyone thinks of you that way. It's clear that you have been working very hard here."

"Oh, well...." I took in a breath, wondering whether I dared mention Lynnis' help. Perhaps I should, if in a roundabout way. "I have made friends with one of the women here," I began. "Lynnis Oakfell, whose husband Hal is also among those who work in the fields."

To my relief, Corin only nodded. "Yes, he had mentioned that his wife had become friendly with you. It makes sense, for she is closest to your age of all the wives here."

"She has become a good friend already," I said. "And she has helped me with puzzling my way through some of these chores. I doubt the food would have been quite as edible as it was without her guidance."

"Ah, so that is the way of it." He smiled and ate a mouthful of the roast chicken. "Then please, send her my compliments. I suppose it is lucky for you that she and Hal don't yet have any children, for she would not have as much time to spare if she did."

Not so lucky for Lynnis and Hal, for I knew

they wanted a family. It was true, though. Without children to look after, the tasks she needed to perform to keep her own small household running were not terribly onerous. And I felt better for having unburdened myself, and having received no condemnation from my husband for accepting someone's help. "Yes, she has been very generous," I said carefully.

"I am glad you have found a friend." He paused then to have another bite of chicken and wash it down with some wine. "Forgive me for my observation, as I did not have any great knowledge of your life before we met, but it seems rather a lonely one, with both your brothers established in estates far away, and no other siblings—especially no sisters. It is good that you have had the chance to meet a young woman of your own age."

I had thought the same thing, but I was warmed that Corin had also noticed, and wished for me to expand my social circle somewhat. "It was lonely," I admitted. "Yes, I had my maid Sendra to talk to, and there was my father, but that is not the same as having a friend of your own age and sex. Once or twice there was some talk of having a cousin come live with us so I might have a companion, but that never seemed to happen. Most of the time I did not mind, for it was not as though I was an utter hermit—we did visit other families, and went to suppers and balls. But I will admit that my situation was not entirely ideal."

"And now?" Corin inquired, giving me another of those penetrating looks.

"Oh, well," I began, then stopped, knowing how much he was able to fluster me, and also knowing that I did not wish to make a rash answer. On the other hand, I did not want to lie. I had done enough of that already. "I am very glad I met Lynnis, and I will admit that the day does go by quickly when one has so much to do. But...."

A lifted eyebrow. "But?"

"But I would not be telling the truth if I said I did not miss my elegant suite back home, or the maids who brought me my bath and did the laundry, or the fine meals the cook prepared every night. And also...." I stopped again, for I was not sure I wanted to reveal one particular matter that had been bothering me, a dissatisfaction I had not even recognized until I began to articulate those details which kept my life from being entirely satisfactory.

"What is it, Marenna? You can tell me."

His tone was soft, almost pleading, his gaze fixed on me. My cheeks heated, and I was glad of the flickering candlelight, for it meant he probably couldn't tell that I had blushed. "It is only that you are gone from dawn 'til past dusk. I am glad that we have a chance to share these dinners, but is this not the time when a newly married couple should get to know one another better? How can we do that when you are hardly here?"

At once he set down his fork and reached across the table so he might rest his hand on mine. It was a strong hand, with well-callused fingers—very unlike the hands of the noblemen I had danced with—but I liked the feeling of wear, for it told me he was not afraid of hard work. "My dear, I know it must be difficult for you. This is all so very different from anything else you have ever known. But you must realize that this current state of affairs will not go on forever. The harvest is a time of heavy labor, it is true. Once the crops are all gathered in, the pace will slow down a good deal."

His words made sense, and yet I could not be entirely relieved by them, for once the harvest was done, we might not have a place here at all, should the man he had temporarily replaced decide he wanted to stay on, rather than face an uncertain future at the onset of winter. "But we do not even know what will happen to us then," I said, my tone subdued.

With one finger, he rubbed the back of my hand, the movement gentle, almost a caress. A small thrill went through me, and I had to take in a breath, make myself focus on what he was about to say. He really was so terribly distracting. "I know the future frightens you, but I think you do not have as much to worry about as you believe you do. Even if Master Threnson decides to reclaim his post once his injury has healed, Master Brinsell has said he is very happy with my work, and will do what he can to make sure we both have a permanent home here. So please, Marenna, set your heart at rest. I do not want you fretting over such a thing when every indication is that we will be happily settled here for years to come."

Those words did calm me somewhat. I tried to envision what life in this cottage would be like come winter...what would happen when I finally allowed myself to be Corin's true wife. Would we have children right away? Such a thing had not happened for Lynnis and her husband, but it seemed they were the exception rather than the rule. I thought this cottage could accommodate one child easily enough, for of course by then I would be sharing the large bedroom with Corin.

Even two might not be so bad. Anything more than that, though, and surely this place would feel as if it was full to bursting.

Oh, I was getting very far ahead of myself. I should just be reassured, and glad to hear that we would not be turned out on the high road once the harvest had been gathered in. There would be cozy evenings by the fireplace and chats with Lynnis as she shared a new recipe with me. Yes, it would all be so very different from everything I was used to, and everything I had expected my life to be, but I thought it would be comfortable enough, once I let go of the past and realized that never again would I ride in a coach and four, or dance the *verdralle* with a small orchestra as accompaniment. Not all joys in life must necessarily be extravagant ones.

"You are very quiet," Corin said. "I thought you would be pleased to hear this news."

"Oh, I am," I responded at once. I certainly did not want him to think I was unhappy at the prospect of staying here in this sanctuary he had found for us. "I suppose I was just thinking of what winter would be like here."

"Somewhat milder than in Silverhold, I would think. Yes, we are only some thirty-five miles south of there, but so close to the mountains, you always received a chill wind in the wintertime. Because Marric's Rest borders the Lozen River and lies in this sheltered valley, it does not bear the brunt of the cold winds and the snowfall that winter brings."

This revelation was also encouraging, because I knew all too well how harsh winters could be in the castle of my birth, how those bleak winds always managed to find their way through every chink in the masonry, every gap in the windows. Even with fires blazing in every hearth, it all too often could be quite uncomfortable. "Well, that is certainly good news."

"You see? All my roaming about has had some benefit, for at least I have a better idea of how the seasons fare in various locations around Sirlende. Of course it would be even warmer in Iselfex, and warmer still down in Delanir where I learned my trade. Indeed, we often received no snow at all there, and I cannot guarantee such a thing here."

Nor would I want it, for I knew that a Midwinter's Eve with no snow would feel odd to me. I told Corin as much, adding, "I enjoy seeing the seasons change. I only would prefer to avoid a blizzard like the one we had last winter, where the castle was so buried that all my father's men took two days to dig us out."

"I think I can safely say that you will not have

to worry about such a thing happening here." He finished the last of the chicken on his plate, and moved to carve another slice from the bird on its platter. "More?"

"Just a little," I replied.

From there we ate and drank quietly, both of us seeming content to be silent as we finished our meal. When we were done, Corin helped me gather up the plates and take them into the kitchen, which was nearly dark, the only illumination the warm-hued crescent moon as it began to rise.

I turned around and bumped into him. An apology sprang to my lips, but I never had a chance to utter it, for he bent and gently placed his mouth against mine.

This was what I had wanted, and yet for a second I froze in shock, so unexpected was his embrace. Then I relaxed into it, let myself taste the tartness of the wine on his lips, allowed myself to revel in the feel of his strong arms around me. His body was so very warm, pressed up against mine.

The kiss did not last as long as I had expected. After a moment, he pulled away slightly, and seemed to be staring down into my face, although the room so dimly lit that I couldn't quite see his expression.

"Do you mind that I did that?"

"'Mind'?" I repeated blankly. Had his kiss bothered me? I supposed it had, but not in the way he probably thought. Heat and chills seemed to alternate in my body, as though I had a fever, and yet I knew I was perfectly healthy. "No—no. Not at all. It was simply...unexpected."

A small silence as he appeared to contemplate my response. "I thought I saw something in your face this evening...something that made me think I might have some luck pressing my suit."

I gave a small, unconvincing chuckle. "Well, I suppose I am getting more used to the thought of being your wife."

"Is that all?"

Of course it wasn't, but I did not know if I had the ability to articulate what I currently was feeling. I'd wanted him to kiss me, but now that he had, it felt as if my body was not my own, as if the touch of his lips on mine had awakened some primal force which had slumbered up until now, waiting for the day when the match of my soul finally arrived.

At the same time, I could not help but think of everything Lynnis had explained to me, what I now knew that Corin wanted. Certainly there was nothing wrong in it—we were husband and wife, and so there would be no shame involved in sharing those intimacies—and yet I still did not know how I should respond to his question.

"I think you know it is not," I said. "I cannot lie to you, Corin. Not about this. I feel...a wakening within me. But with everything that has changed in my life, I still am not sure."

"You are not sure of me?"

His voice had been carefully neutral, but I thought I still detected the hurt within it. "No," I replied. "I am not sure of myself."

He reached out to me, pulled me close. His lips brushed against my hair, and he said, "It is all right, my darling. I understand. I told you before that you might take as much time as you need, and I am telling you that again. It is enough to know that you did not mind me kissing you. It is a first step."

"A step I welcome." I paused, then said quickly, "So kiss me again, Corin."

Which he did, his mouth seeking mine, all the strength and goodness and passion within him seeming to come with that touch of lip on lip. And as much as I reveled in that embrace, some part of me wanted to weep as well, for I did not know what was wrong with me.

Why could I not allow myself to be his wife in more than name?

CHAPTER 9

THE NEXT DAY PASSED, AND ANOTHER, AND another. Each night Corin and I sat down to dinner, and spoke of our days, and kissed one another good night. I know he was waiting for me to tell him that I no longer wanted to sleep in the narrow bed I had taken for my own, and join him in the bedroom that should have been ours, but still my reluctance prevented me from granting him that wish. Lynnis hinted around the problem, but, for all her seeming boldness, she apparently was not daring enough to ask me point-blank whether I had taken her advice and submitted to my husband's most intimate caresses.

And yes, it seemed that what Corin had told me about his future here was only the truth, because even though the grape harvest was now over, no one asked him to leave. Indeed, Master Brinsell requested that he assist in organizing the crush, for not only was it the time when all the women came out to mash the grapes, but there would also be a celebration afterward, with tables set out among the trees and all manner of food and drink. At least I knew I would be able to relax somewhat, for in answer to my somewhat tentative question, Lynnis informed me that the duke did not attend the crush, but instead waited to honor the harvest with a grand feast and ball at the castle. Thank the gods for that, as I did not think I could manage having him see me in such an undignified position.

By that point, I still could not claim to be a very accomplished cook, but I was good at following directions, and that was all Anisa, one of the older women who could no longer crush the grapes, required. She watched over me as I helped make platter after platter of sausage rolls and pasties and breads both savory and sweet. Lynnis also assisted in this task, and it seemed by the time we were done, we had enough food to feed an army.

Tables were set up among the grove that bordered the fields, and the men put out lanterns on poles, for it appeared that the party was intended to last far into the nighttime hours. The women covered the tables in cloths, and everyone brought out the stoneware from their households so we would have ample plates and platters and goblets.

Once all the preparations were done, the women gathered at the scene of the crush itself. Four enormous tubs were set out on the grass, and a large canopy stretched overhead to protect the vulnerable grapes from passing birds. Lynnis showed me how to tie up my skirts to get them out of the way—and oh, how I blushed to be revealing not just my ankles, but my legs nearly up to my knees—and then helped me climb into one of the vats.

The grapes felt strange under my bare feet, oddly bouncy and slippery. I clung to the edge of the tub and waited for my friend to join me, even as I tried my best to avoid the amused glances of the men, who had gathered around the tubs, most of them already drinking from the bottles of wine that had been set out on the tables. Most everyone looked on this as only fair, since it was the men who had done the hard work up until this point. Now it was their time to relax and enjoy themselves.

"Go on," Lynnis said, since she had just entered the tub herself. She reached up to touch her hair, which was tightly braided against her scalp. I had done the same thing, to keep any stray strands from falling into the crush. "Up and down. Like you're walking, but with a little more force."

Reluctantly, I let go of the edge of the tub and took one hesitant step. The grapes seemed to roll beneath my feet rather than being smashed, and I wondered what on earth would happen if I lost my balance and fell face first into the crush. No, I could not allow that to happen. In the past, I had been praised as a very good dancer, and I tried to recall those skills now, the balance and the lightness of foot. I certainly would not allow myself to be defeated by a vat full of grapes.

I stomped down with one foot and then the other, trying to make a little game of it. A few feet away from me, Lynnis laughed and tossed her head. "Yes, that's the way of it!" she said. "You are so slender that you probably have to exert a little more force than the rest of us, but it seems that you are beginning to get your rhythm."

And so I was. I hopped from one foot to the other, moving around, trying to make sure I did not miss any sections in the tub. From off to one side, I heard the sound of a viol playing a lively tune, and I craned my head to see who it might be. To my surprise, the musician turned out to be

Master Brinsell himself, a smile on his face and a twinkle in his dark eyes. The watching men began to clap, and those of us standing in our vats of grapes began to stomp along in time with the music.

A laugh escaped my lips. I simply couldn't help myself, for I could not remember the last time I had felt so silly, so lighthearted and free. No doubt if anyone from my former life could have seen me, their laughter would have been of the scornful sort, and they would have mocked me for getting dirty with the peasants. But it wasn't like that at all. Yes, these people had work that needed to be done, but they had changed it into almost a game, something to be looked forward to rather than dreaded.

Around and around Lynnis and I went, both of us giggling like two girls still back in the schoolroom. I kept catching flashes of Corin as he stood off to the side and watched us. He, like most of the men, wore a smile, but I could see something else in his expression beyond mere amusement. It looked almost like surprise, as if he had not expected me to relax into this activity the way I had. But then, how could he have known about the strictures that had ruled my life up until a few short days ago? I was always admonished to keep my voice low and soft, to not laugh too loudly, to move with elegance and grace, and never admit to anything less than perfection. All those rules were so ingrained in women of my class that I had stopped thinking about them long before, but now I could see how hemmed in I had been, trammeled like a wild thing in a cage.

Here, no one cared for any of those niceties. The men laughed, but they were laughing with us rather than at us, were pleased to see us making this necessary chore into something of a romp. Not a one of them had leered at our exposed legs—of course, I did not think anyone would find them particularly attractive now, not splashed with dark juice up to the knees as they were.

After Master Brinsell had played a good set of four tunes, he came over to the tub where Lynnis and I were still stomping gamely away, and bent down and inspected the crushed grapes within. "You have done a fine job here, my ladies," he said. "I think you can stop now and reward your-selves with a cup of wine."

That did sound like a good reward, for although I would have kept gamely at the task for as long as he needed us to, I was beginning to be rather wearied and was glad to be given permis-sion to stop. Both Corin and Hal came over to the vat and helped to lift Lynnis and me out. It was a good thing that Hal was a big man, sturdy and broad-shouldered, for someone slighter than he might have had a difficult time hoisting his tall and well-built wife.

One of the ladies who was too elderly to participate in the crush came over with a jug of water and some clean cloths, so we might wipe down our legs and feet. Then it was time to put our shoes and stockings back on, and go over to the tables, where we sat and allowed ourselves to be waited on by our husbands.

"I believe I could get used to this," Lynnis murmured to me as Hal handed her a sturdy earthenware cup, full almost to the rim with new wine.

For that was the tradition at the estate, that during this harvest celebration, the vintners would open the barrels of the wine set out the year before and sample it. This gave everyone a good idea of how well it was aging, for Corin had told me that it depended on the grape and the vintage, and sometimes the wine would be bottled immediately afterward, and other times it would be sent back to age for another year, or possibly even two.

He handed me my cup, and I drank. Yes, I could tell the wine was still young, for it had a sharpness upon first taste that I guessed age would help to mellow, but underneath that I could taste the richness of the fruit, the nuances of this particular vintage.

"So, Mistress Blackstone," Master Brinsell said as he approached us. "What say you? Another year in the barrel, or two?"

I glanced over at Corin, who gave me an encouraging nod. "Well," I replied, then took another sip. "I certainly do not profess to be an expert, but I think that there is a complexity here which could do with two years in the barrel—if, of course, you can afford to be so patient."

The two men exchanged a glance, Master Brinsell's lips quirking slightly. However, when he spoke, his tone was sober enough, as if he wanted to make sure I knew that he was giving my suggestion ample thought. "Oh, mistress, you do not need to worry whether the duke can afford to keep this wine aging for another year. While his vineyards do bring in a good income, the duchy certainly does not need them to survive. Growing vines is an amusement to him, a diversion. It will not matter whether he keeps this wine in barrels for two more years—or five, should it come to that."

I supposed I should have guessed as much, for it had become clear to me that Lord

Sorthannic did not appear to want for anything...
and, unlike many other rich men, he did not
clutch his wealth tightly to himself, but made
sure it was used to keep the people on his estates
comfortable. Even so, I could not quite prevent a
certain sharpness from entering my tone as I
said, "Indeed? If the vineyards are such a diversion, I wonder that he does not come down here
himself to observe the crush. I would think it
might amuse him."

Once again Corin and Master Brinsell looked
at one another. For a moment, I feared that I had
been too impertinent, and that my husband
might take me to task for speaking in such a way
of our lord and master. However, he only smiled
and shook his head, saying, "No, he regards this
as our little celebration, and would not think to
intrude. He has Master Brinsell to report back to
him on how the crush fared, and that is all he
requires."

"Yes, and remember that he will be hosting a
great harvest ball a week from now anyway, with
all the grand ladies and gentlemen from the
surrounding estates in attendance," Lynnis put
in. "So he certainly has no need to come and
watch our rustic amusements."

"I don't think they're rustic," I protested,
looking around at all the people present, their

smiling faces, the brightly colored flags hanging from the trees, the torches that had just been lit, for the sun was beginning to sink low in the sky. "I think it's all lovely."

"And she has had only a few sips of wine," Corin said, dark eyes glinting with mischief. "So you know she is telling the simple truth."

Several retorts sprang to my mind, but because I knew he was teasing me, I settled for sticking my tongue out at him in a most unlady-like manner. I was sure that Sendra, had she been there to witness my behavior, would have fainted dead away from shock.

But Corin only laughed, then said he would fetch us our dinner. Hal joined in, and the three men walked away to the refreshments table so they might load up some plates with food for us.

"Yes, this would be a good way to live," Lynnis said. "To have someone wait on you at all times, to never have to lift a finger to do anything you did not want to do."

"Oh, I would think even that would become tiresome after a while," I replied. "For there is a certain pride that comes from doing things for oneself. Besides, if you had someone who waited on you hand and foot, you would never have learnt all the practical skills you have now. Why, look at how ignorant I was, and that was only because my stepmother did not wish to teach me anything. I am much more content at the end of the day now, knowing that I have accomplished something worthwhile in taking care of my household."

"You may have a point." She was silent for a moment, watching the men as they joked with one another, good-naturedly squabbling over which of them would bring his wife the choicest morsels from the food laid out before them. "Still, I think it would be quite grand to live like that just for a short time—say, a week or so, just to have a little space of time in which to rest. I do not think that would be enough to spoil me for all future domestic endeavors."

"No, I suppose it would not," I agreed. "It would only be enough to allow you to relax, and to have more energy when you did return to your usual life."

"And it gives me something to dream of," she added. "I know such a thing will never come to pass, but it is pleasant to think about."

Corin and Hal approached us then, both of them carrying plates so loaded with food that I was secretly surprised some of it had not spilled over the edges as they made their way across the glade to us. Lynnis and I shifted on our benches so the men could sit down, and the feasting commenced.

It was such simple food compared to what I was used to, and yet it tasted better than anything I had eaten for a long time. Perhaps it was only my exertions from earlier that lent the dishes an extra spice, or perhaps it was sitting outdoors, feeling the fresh breeze ruffle across my tightly braided hair. Those soft breezes brought with them the scent of warm grass and dried leaves, and a faint, sweet-sour tang I thought must come from the vats of crushed grapes themselves.

All around us, people ate and laughed and talked, and Lynnis and Hal and Corin and I did the same, discussing the harvest, discussing the prospects for the winter ahead—would it be mild, or harsh?—talking of Master Brinsell's announcement that the duke planned to have five more cottages built here in our little settlement, so he might lure more workers next spring to help expand the duke's already extensive fields and vineyards.

It was a pleasant time, and I found myself sated soon enough, my head leaning against Corin's sturdy shoulder as he and Hal argued the merits of planting *larsonne* grapes on the upslope parcel where Lord Sorthannic intended to extend the vineyard, or whether the *siris* grape could manage the sandier soil there. The conversation became quite technical, and I realized I wasn't listening to the content of their discussion any longer, but merely enjoying the sound of their voices, especially Corin's warm baritone. My eyelids fluttered, and I knew I was very close to dozing off. Not that surprising, I supposed, after being out in the warm sun and exerting myself in such a way, and then eating and drinking so very much.

Corin tapped my shoulder, and I startled. "It is far too early to be sleepy, my wife," he said. "Look, Master Brinsell has his viol out, and Trey is going to play his drum. Now that the sun has set, it is time to dance."

Indeed, when I blinked and looked around, I saw that several couples had already gathered in a clear area where the grass had been beaten down to the bare earth. It was not quite the same as the grand ballroom in my father's castle, with its wrought-iron chandeliers and polished wooden floors, but I supposed it would do well enough.

I let Corin take me by the hand and help me up from the bench, then lead me over to stand with the other dancers. Once again, a little thrill went through me at his touch, although this time I knew there was nothing truly intimate about it.

At the same time, I could not help but be slightly nervous. Yes, some country dances were included in my repertoire, along with far more courtly ones such as the *verdralle* and the *linotte*, and yet I could not know for sure whether the people here would perform those country dances in the same way that I had been taught.

Well, I told myself, *you were always counted a quick study on the dance floor, so if they are slightly different, you should not have too much difficulty learning how to go along.*

I also had to hope that Corin was a competent dancer. This was the first time we'd had the opportunity to participate in such an activity, and so I had no idea whether he was the epitome of grace, or someone possessed of two left feet.

Well, I supposed I would find out soon enough.

Within minutes, we had enough people gathered in the little clear area to make up a circle. The men stood on the outside facing in, while the women made up a smaller circle facing out. Master Brinsell played a few chords on his viol, and Trey tapped on his drum, and then the music began in earnest, with all of us joining hands with our partners and moving first to the left, then to the right.

This was the "Bannot Bar," a very old dance,

one of the first I had ever learnt. Nothing about how it was danced this night was very different from what I had been taught, and so I found myself relaxing slightly. The only pity of it was that one changed partners with every chorus, the two concentric circles moving in opposite directions, and so I did not have much opportunity to truly dance with my husband.

Perhaps that was for the best. I knew they would probably not dance the *verdralle,* and so I would not have to worry about spending an entire dance with his arm around my waist, and my hand clasped in his. I already had a difficult time controlling my reactions around him, and if he proved to be proficient in that courtly dance, it would be that much harder to remain calm and not allow myself to be carried away by his mere presence.

Would that be such a bad thing? I wondered, and did not know if I had the courage to answer the question. Corin and I had been growing closer each day, but still I found myself reticent, not able to take that final step toward being his wife. One might argue that it had not been all that long, that we had not been married even a week yet. However, I knew I could not keep up this very different kind of dance with him indefinitely.

The next piece was the very lively "Black Nag," and Lynnis and I switched partners for that one, all of us laughing as we tried to keep up with the ever-increasing pace of the music. Afterward, I begged off, saying I needed to rest for a bit. This was nothing more than the truth, for I was still wearing my bedraggled slippers, as we had not had the opportunity to acquire a new pair of shoes for me yet. Even though the ground was flat and even and free of stones, it was hard enough on those slippers, which had never been intended for this kind of treatment.

Corin did not seem to mind sitting out, however, and went to fetch me more wine as I sat down in my former place on one of the benches. A few others were also resting after the exertions of "Black Nag," but they were involved in their own conversations, ignoring me. Not in an unfriendly way, of course, only talking with their partners, or their neighbors, rather than someone who was still very much a newcomer to their settlement.

I smiled at my husband as he brought me my wine, then sat down next to me. "Are you enjoying yourself?" he inquired.

"Very much so." I sipped some wine, then lifted my head to gaze up at the heavens, brightly spangled with stars, a waxing yellow moon just barely visible through the oak trees that stood to the east of the little glade. The torches flickered and danced in the breeze, which by now was much cooler. However, I barely felt it, still warmed by the dancing I had just done. "It is so beautiful out here in the night air." I hesitated and looked around, but no one seemed to be paying any attention to us, or what we were saying. "I wonder why my father never held a dance outdoors in the summer, for I must confess that the ballroom could get very stuffy in warm weather."

"Ah, well, dancing outside is for peasants, I suppose."

Was it my imagination, or was there a note of subtle condemnation in his tone? Possibly, although I didn't think it was directed at me. Because I was having such a pleasant evening, I decided to let it go. "The peasants have the right of it in this, I think. Of course, such an event would not be possible in the wintertime, but it is good to enjoy this weather while it lasts."

Corin nodded and drank some of the wine in his cup. I really had not been paying attention, and so I did not know for sure how much he had consumed this evening. Probably at least three cupfuls, for of course the men had started early, had begun to drink their wine while I and the rest of the women who were up to the task had still been stomping around in those vats full of grapes. However, he did not seem any the worse for wear, or unsteady at all; I had attended enough parties where some of the men in attendance had over-indulged to recognize the signs and was glad not to see any of that in my husband. Sometimes men could get so unruly when they were in their cups.

Several more dances were played, and then Master Brinsell played the first chords of the *polshare*, a first cousin to the *verdralle*. It was not quite as breathless, but required some of the same proximity to one's partner. Corin set his cup down on the table and rose, extending a hand. "Let us dance this one."

I did not dare refuse. To tell the truth, I did not want to decline his invitation, even though I trembled a bit at the thought of him holding me close throughout the length of the dance. I set down my own cup and stood, and let him take me over to the impromptu dance floor. He pulled me close, and I had to draw in a breath at his nearness. We did not spend much time thus, so I had to tell myself to remain calm, to not allow him to see how much the feel of his arm around my waist, his hand in mine, made my heart pound in my chest.

There were not as many dancers for this one, possibly because they were already wearied, or possibly because they did not know it as well as some of the more rustic dances. I noticed that Lynnis and Hal chose to sit down, her head pillowed on his shoulder, their hands clasped together. They always seemed so easy and comfortable with one another, and I hoped that one day Corin and I would share that same kind of friendly intimacy.

But then I had no thought for anything except the steps of the dance, the way we wove in and out with the other couples participating, the pressure of Corin's hand on my waist. In that moment, I wished we might be alone so I could lift my face to him and he could kiss me again, those kisses that inflamed me simply because they were so cautious. Always I had the sense of him holding back, and knew that my own reluctance and inexperience must be the cause of his reticence. What would it be like if he truly let go?

No, it was better not to contemplate such things while in the company of others. We swirled around and around, and the stars glittered overhead, and the smoke from the torches filled the air with its sharp, aromatic tang. When the dance was over, I laid my head against Corin's shoulder, just as I had seen Lynnis doing with her own husband. It did feel good to feel his strength, to know that this man was mine and no one else's.

We applauded Master Brinsell and Trey's playing, and walked toward the benches. Corin lowered his head to my ear and murmured, "Shall we go home?"

I wanted to, very much. At the same time, anxiety stirred within me. After such an evening, I was not sure what might happen next.

But I nodded, saying, "Yes, let us go home."

We walked away from the company. I noticed we were not the only ones to slip off at that point, as though everyone had begun to recognize that the party was winding down. Corin twined his fingers in mine, helping to guide me through the uncertain moonlight to the back door of our cottage.

Within, all was quite dark. However, I always left a candlestick in its pewter holder on the countertop there, along with a box of matches. I reached for it, letting go of my husband's hand so I might strike a match and light the candle.

He let out a breath as I did so, although I could not be quite sure whether that was from annoyance at my letting go of him, or because he did not think we needed the illumination. However, he did not say anything, only stood there for a moment, staring down at me. Then, still without speaking, he reached up and pulled at the pins in my hair, letting the braids fall to my shoulders. His fingers worked at the plaits until my hair was freed, lying in a wavy mass over my shoulders.

"There," he said, his voice a husky whisper. "That is better."

I supposed it probably was; the hairstyle had been chosen for its practicality, not its loveliness. But there had been something intimate, something tender, about the way he loosened my hair, taking a liberty that no one save my husband might. "It would have gotten in the way," I pointed out, not sure why I had bothered to state something so obvious, except that speaking of such commonplaces seemed like a way to lessen some of the tension I could feel building between us.

"Yes," he replied. "But it is not in the way now." He reached up and passed a hand over my hair, the caress very gentle.

And yet I could feel the way his fingers trembled.

"You are so beautiful," he whispered. "When I first laid eyes on you, I realized I had never seen a woman so beautiful."

Blood rushed to my cheeks, but I managed to

lightly say, "Indeed? For I seem to recall a comment about being 'rather comely.'"

"I was referring to your portrait, not to you. It did you no justice at all."

How should I reply to that remark? And how should I react to these bold-faced paeans to my beauty? More than once I had caught Corin gazing at me and thought that perhaps he admired me more than he had spoken of aloud, and yet I was still not quite prepared for such open admiration.

"I never thought much of that painter," I said. "But Father insisted on hiring him."

"Your father should have listened to you."

But then Corin seemed to decide speech was no longer necessary, for he bent his face to mine, kissed me in a way I had never experienced before—his arms tight around me, his lips insistent on mine. I tasted wine on his lips, sensed his loose hair brushing against my cheek. I felt as though I was drowning, and yet somehow, I had no desire to fight my way back to dry land.

After an interminable moment, one that seemed as if it should have been counted in centuries rather than in seconds, he let go of me and stepped away. His chest rose and fell as though he had just run a race, and he passed a hand through his hair.

"My apologies, my wife."

I stared at him, startled. What in the world was he apologizing for? The gods only knew that he had kissed me before now.

But none of those kisses were like this one, I thought. *Something has changed, although I am not sure what.*

"It was a very good kiss," I told him. "I did not mind it at all."

"Yes, but I swore to myself—" He broke off there, as if realizing he was about to reveal something he had intended to keep to himself. "It is no matter. It is late, and you should go to sleep."

The way he said those words made it clear that he wished me to go to sleep in my room, rather than join him in his. Only a few hours earlier, I would have been relieved by such an intention, but now I was not sure what I thought. The wine had mellowed me, and the dances we had shared had told me that we already knew one another's rhythms. For the first time, I thought I might be brave enough to let him make me his.

Unfortunately, it appeared as though he was having second thoughts.

"If that is what you wish, Corin," I said.

"What I wish—" Again he stopped himself. "I am not sure what I wish. Good night, Marenna."

Before I could open my mouth to protest, he had turned from me and walked out of the kitchen. Sadly, I knew there was nothing I could to do to stop him.

Repressing a sigh, I bent down and blew out the candle.

CHAPTER 10

ONCE AGAIN CORIN WAS GONE WHEN I AWOKE THE next morning. I would have wondered at his absence, since now that the harvest was done, he did not have to be up before dawn...except I was fairly certain he did not wish to encounter me first thing, and so had left before we had a chance to see one another.

Cowardly? Perhaps. And yet I thought I could understand something of why he had behaved in such a way. When I awoke, I lay in bed for a long while, staring at the ceiling and attempting to determine what I should say to him when he came home. Possibly the wisest course of action was to say nothing at all. I had been ready, when suddenly he was not—it seemed that we would always be at cross-purposes.

No, not always. I had to remind myself that I had shared this cottage with him for only a week now. While some might say that was ample time for us to work through our differences, I knew better. He had been patient with me, and so I needed to do him the courtesy of showing him that same patience.

If only I could understand what he had meant when he said he had sworn something to himself. Had he made a vow not to touch me until he knew I was ready? Perhaps, but one would have thought I had given him ample indication last night that I was.

Apparently not.

Lynnis had informed me that I would be required to help with the clean-up this morning —only not at a very early hour, since it was expected that most people would sleep late after their indulgences of the night before. All the same, I did not tarry too long while I washed my face and got dressed, nor did I spend much time over breakfast. My appetite was not what it might have been, and so I had only a slice of toast and an apple before heading out to see where I was needed.

The vats of crushed grapes had disappeared. Corin had mentioned once or twice that Lord Sorthannic's castle possessed vast cellars, and I assumed that was where the crush had been taken to be stored. Likewise, the canopies that had protected the precious grapes were also gone. However, all the tables and benches remained, as well as the platters and wine cups. The leftover food—if there had been any—must have been packaged up the night before by those who remained on the scene until the very end.

Lynnis approached me, yawning and scratching at the back of her neck. Her entire person seemed rather bleary, and I wondered how late she had stayed up the night before.

"You seem brighter-eyed than most of us this morning," she remarked, and I lifted my shoulders.

"Ah, well, we did not stay quite as late as some of you." I went over to one of the erstwhile food tables and began stacking empty platters and plates and cups.

"True." She came up beside me and began to help with gathering up the discarded serving ware. As she leaned forward, I spied a bright red mark on the side of her neck.

Evidence that she and Hal had not gone directly to sleep once they got home?

The thought made me blush, and I averted my eyes, pretending to be intent on the task in front of me. Once I had cleared the table, however, I said, "I thought with the harvest done, the men would not have to be up and about so early."

She straightened and sent me a quizzical glance, as though attempting to determine if there was any subtext to my comment. Apparently she found none, for she replied, "The grape harvest is over, but the wheat fields are vast, and help is needed there as well. They will work on those for the next few days, and then yes, once that crop is gathered in, they will not have to be up and about quite as early."

I supposed I should have thought of that. Yes, Corin's experience made him particularly invaluable in the grape harvest, but he possessed a strong back and quick hands, so it was only natural that he would be expected to lend his assistance to the gathering of another crop. "Oh, of course. I should have thought of that."

"Are you missing him?"

I saw nothing but honest curiosity in her expression. Well, on this point, I could be truthful enough. Corin certainly knew how I felt about the long hours he had been working. "Yes, I suppose so. It is difficult to start out one's life with one's partner so absent. I know he is only doing this to make sure we have a secure future, but at the same time, I am looking forward to winter, when he will not have as much to do."

She chuckled. "I believe that is the first time I have ever heard anyone say they looked forward to wintertime, although I can see why you would feel that way. But perhaps you will feel differently when you have both been cooped up in your cottage for days because the snow is piled up all around, and it is not safe even to go out to hunt."

"I thought the winters were milder here?"

"Milder than what?" Lynnis shrugged, then went on without waiting for an answer. "I suppose north of here it can be much worse, but we still have more than our fair share of snow. But the hunting can be good, even in the winter."

"And Lord Sorthannic does not forbid it on his lands?" My father had always been lax about such things, but I had heard of other lords who would banish those who dared to hunt on land that belonged to the nobility.

"Oh, no." She picked up a stack of platters and moved them to a cart one of the other women had set off to the side, so that they could all be wheeled away and washed once the tables had been cleared. "I know that is not the custom, but his Grace cares little for custom—I suppose because he was not raised to it. So everyone is free to hunt rabbits and deer and ducks and grouse, or to fish in the streams that cross his lands, although sometimes they do freeze over. Why, he even has a great hunt at midwinter where he invites all the men on the estate to attend. They go on foot, rather than on horse-back, for of course the workers don't have their own mounts. Hal has come back from those hunts with enough game to last us for weeks, so of course it is very much appreciated."

I was silent for a moment, considering her words. Truly it did seem that Lord Sorthannic was a gracious and noble lord to his tenants, and once again I inwardly chastised myself for treating him so ill. Not that I did not care for Corin—of course I did—but I could not help but think how different my life would be if I had accepted the duke's suit, rather than mocking his appearance.

"You are very quiet," Lynnis observed as she planted her hands on her hips and sent me a searching glance. "What occupies your mind?"

"Oh, nothing, really." I tilted my head at her. "Does Lord Sorthannic ever come here to our little settlement? It is true that he seems to be a most generous lord, but he also seems rather, well, detached from everything."

For a moment, she said nothing. Indeed, for almost the first time since I had met her, she seemed somewhat ill at ease. Then she lifted her chin and gave a forced little chuckle. "Oh, he comes by from time to time, but generally not at this time of year, for he is very busy with the harvest. Our work with the grapes is done, but he likes to personally oversee the transfer of the crush to the barrels, and so forth. He does always visit in the spring, so he can inspect the cottages for himself and make sure that any necessary repairs are carried out."

This seemed to make sense, so I was not sure why she should appear so uneasy before she made her reply. Perhaps she had thought I was criticizing the duke for being so absent. On the contrary; my life had been made so much easier by not having to worry about avoiding him. It could be that I was entirely puffing up my own importance, and he would not even recall who I was if our paths did happen to cross, but I did not want to put that particular hypothesis to the test.

And really, it would not be so strange if he did not recognize me, dressed plainly as I was, with my hair braided out of the way most days, my hands already beginning to turn rough from all the daily chores I must manage. The only time Lord Sorthannic had ever seen me, I had been wearing a sumptuous silk gown, and my hair had fallen in perfectly formed ringlets over my shoulders, thanks to hours of work by Sendra as I sat in front of the hearth and she repeatedly placed the curling iron in the fire to heat it back up again.

Thinking of all that pampering, and of the smoothness of silk against my skin, I could not help but let out a small sigh.

"Are you quite all right, Marenna?" Lynnis asked, and now I thought I saw true concern in her hazel eyes.

"Oh, yes. I suppose I am just tired. Although I did not stay awake particularly late, still it was a rather strenuous afternoon and evening. But today promises to be rather a quiet day, so I see no reason why I should not recover quickly."

She nodded, although I noticed she still looked rather troubled. I thought it entirely possible that she had hoped Corin and I would finally become close, after such a romantic evening of dancing and wine drinking. However, since I had said I did not stay up late, she probably guessed at the truth, and realized that nothing in the current state of affairs had changed very much.

After that, though, it was time to take all the dirty plates over to Anisa's house, for she possessed the largest kitchen. With so many hands pitching in, we made short work of the task. Not that we were done, of course. Now that the tables and been cleared and the dishes washed and dispersed to the various households whence they had come, it was time to wash all the cloths that had covered the tables, and to pick up whatever litter might remain in the area. We did not move the tables themselves, as the men would do that once they returned after their day's work.

And I still had to do my own laundering, and a dinner to make. By the time dusk began to steal over the landscape, I was feeling wearier than I thought I ever had before. The work slipped by so much more easily when it was shared with another, but Lynnis had her own domestic tasks to attend to, and I did not feel comfortable begging once more for her help. After all, I had been here for more than a week. While I could not say I was a master of any of the innumerable chores required to keep our household running smoothly, I had acquired enough skills to ensure that I probably wouldn't botch anything too badly, even when left to my own devices.

Corin returned just as I was pulling the chicken pie I had made out of the oven. No more grape stains, but he was still dusty and dirty, and also appeared more wearied by his day's labors than he had been when he was working with the vines.

Well, it is not that much of a mystery, I told myself as I greeted him and told him dinner would be on the table soon. *For he also danced and drank last night, and yet had to go out in the fields. Also, this is not work that he loves. He is only doing it because he must. It is always more tiring to do something you have no passion for.*

Even so, he summoned a smile for me as he sat down at the dinner table, and sniffed appreciatively at the pie while I cut him a large slice and put it on his plate. I had not set out any wine, and I noticed that he did not ask for it. Possibly he had realized we were consuming it too quickly...or he had decided that he'd had enough the night before. I was somewhat relieved, for drinking too much wine had led me to lose my control, and I did not want a repeat of that experience.

Or possibly it was not the losing control that bothered me, but the memory of the way I had been rebuffed by my own husband.

We ate in silence for a moment; I could tell he did not wish to talk. Just as well, for I was having a difficult time deciding what I should say to him. The awkwardness of our first few days together had come rushing back, and I did not know what to do about it. Before Corin, my only interactions with men had involved the empty pleasantries exchanged while seated at the banquet table, or on the dance floor. I was not yet comfortable with speaking the truth of my heart.

At last he said, "I saw that everything from our little gala last night has already been cleaned up."

A nice neutral topic. "Yes," I replied. "For of course everyone needed to reclaim their dishes, and Lorissa's leg—the one with rheumatism in her knee—was paining her, which she swears means rain is coming. I am not entirely certain of that, for the weather has been very fine, but...."

"Lorissa's knee is as good a prediction as anything else," Corin said. "The men say she is right almost three-quarters of the time, which seems like a good reason for making sure all the tables and so forth have been put away."

Perhaps she would be proved correct. I reflected that it was a good thing the harvest had gone off so well, and so quickly. I did not know much about farming, but I did know that rain was not a good thing when crops were being gathered in. The wet could make them rot in the granaries, and that was the last thing any of us needed, although I supposed Lord Sorthannic was rich enough to purchase enough grain to get the estate through the winter, should it come to that.

Usually I enjoyed rain, the sound of it pattering against the windows of my father's castle, the rich smells of wet earth and stone and grass. Now, though, I could only think of it as the first sign that these warm early autumn days would be over before we knew it, and we would soon move on to the darkness of winter.

"Well, if Lorissa's knee turns out to be correct, then we will all feel that much happier about getting everything cleaned up so quickly," I remarked, my tone light. Already enough tension existed between Corin and myself, and I did not want my worry about winter coming to reveal itself in my voice or my expression.

He nodded and toyed with his fork for a moment, playing with a bit of pie crust. Normally, he was not given to those sorts of nervous gestures, and I wondered what might be preying on his mind. Had Master Brinsell told him he would not be staying on as the under-overseer after all?

My stomach lurched, and I reached for my cup so I might drink some water. That helped to calm it somewhat, but my nerves still felt edgy and raw, like harp strings for the wind to play on.

Corin set down his fork. "Master Brinsell had some news for me today."

"Oh?"

"Yes. He said that he would like to have me continue my duties as under-overseer."

The rush of relief that went over me was so intense, I felt drained afterward. Thank the gods. So all my worrying had been for naught.

However, the next word Corin uttered brought all my worries rushing back. "But...."

"But what?"

He pushed a loose lock of hair behind one ear, and although he looked across the table at me, I had the impression that his gaze was fixed on something else...all because he could not meet my eyes. "He said that I will not have a great deal to do over the next few months, but that perhaps you could help."

"I?" I repeated, not sure what he was driving at. "How on earth can I help with making wine?"

"You misunderstand me. It is not that you would be helping me, but rather if you took on some additional duties, then you could be seen as contributing enough that our staying here in this cottage would be justified."

I did not bother to keep the suspicion out of my voice. "What kind of duties are we talking about?"

"One of the kitchen maids in the castle has just borne her first child, and so she can no longer perform her work. Master Brinsell suggested that you go to the castle's kitchen and take over her duties. That way, the steward will not have to hire anyone else, and you will make it so we are not staying here on sufferance."

A kitchen maid. In the very castle of the man who had asked me to be his wife. Surely this could not be happening! No, I was having a nightmare, one of those terrible dreams where you see yourself dancing at a ball while clad only in your underthings, or you wake up miles from home with no good idea of how you got there.

"You cannot be asking this of me, Corin," I said in barely more than a whisper. "I cannot do such a thing."

He stared at me in some consternation, clearly confused as to why I should be so adamantly opposed to the notion. "Why on earth not? Very well, I suppose I can see why you would think such a post would be beneath someone of your station. But you have done much the same work here, with nary a complaint. Indeed, I have been most impressed by how quickly you have adapted."

"That is different," I protested. "You are my husband. Of course it is my duty to do these things for you, because you are my husband, and this is my home. But to go be a servant in the duke's castle—I do not think I can bear the idea!"

His dark eyes glinted, and I realized he was beginning to be angry. Still, his voice was even enough as he said, "Marenna, it is honest work. Master Lewyn, the steward, is a good man, and Brynna, the cook—who rules the kitchens—is not the sort of woman who would allow anything bad to happen to you while you work there."

"But...." My voice was a piteous whisper, and I swallowed, then told myself to not be a coward. "But it is beneath me, Corin."

At once I knew I had said the wrong thing, for his eyes narrowed, and his lips thinned. "Spoken like the spoiled daughter of a baron that you are. Let me tell you, Marenna, that it would be a great deal more beneath you to be turned out of this cottage, to walk the high road in the wintertime with no prospect of permanent shelter."

Although I knew he was correct on some level, I could not allow myself to be spoken to in such a way. I pushed myself up out of my chair and said, "I will not do it."

"Oh, yes, you will." He stood as well, and I realized how tall and strong and somehow fore-boding he was, how, if he wished to, he could make me do anything he wanted.

And how he had not. He had shown forbearance, and patience, when he could have forced
me, whether or not I was ready. No, I did not like
being called spoiled, but I also could not
completely deny that epithet, either. I hated the
very idea of having to work in the castle's kitchen,
but if my own stubbornness and pride allowed us
to lose this comfortable little home we had made
together, I knew I would never forgive myself.

"I will not—I will not have to serve any of the
food, will I?" Somehow I thought I might be able
to bear it if I knew I could hide in the kitchen the
entire time, with no chance of the duke or
anyone who came to visit him ever seeing me.

"No, of course not. Lord Sorthannic has
footmen who wait on him, and serve at his
dinner parties, just as you must have had in your
own household. Or had you forgotten that minor
point of etiquette?"

In my terror, I truly had. I had already
conjured up gruesome images of being sent out
to the duke's dining room, platter of food in
hand, and being forced to set it down directly in
front of him. His eyes would meet mine, and
recognition would dawn...and then he would
begin to laugh, and point, and tell everyone
present that I had once been the Baron of Silver-

hold's daughter, now brought low by my foolish tongue and overweening pride.

Of course I knew that Lord Sorthannic would not do anything so cruel, no matter what I might have said to him in the past. Everything everyone had told me about his behavior as lord of this estate proved him to be a good man, just and loyal and generous. But it was so easy to believe the worst.

"Yes, I suppose I did," I replied. My fingers found the edge of the table and clung to it, as if I needed its steadying stability to prevent me from falling down then and there. Even if I were allowed to hide in the kitchen and never be seen by the duke or any of his grand guests, I still did not look forward to this next stage of my life at all. I took in a breath, then asked, "For how long?"

"How long?"

"How long will I be expected to be a kitchen drudge?" I snapped. "For surely you cannot expect me to toil away in such a demeaning fashion forever."

A moment earlier, his expression had begun to soften, but now his jaw hardened again. "For the winter, I expect. Once I am working dawn to dusk again, I would think that Master Brinsell and Master Lewyn will deem I am pulling my full weight."

From his tone, I could tell he was being ironic. Still, I decided to take his words at face value. "Very well, then. Through the winter, if I must. But once the snows have melted and you are at work in the fields again, Lord Sorthannic will have to find himself a new scullery maid."

"Kitchen maid," Corin corrected me. "You will be helping to prepare the meals, not doing any of the scrubbing or washing-up. That should help to set your heart at ease."

"Oh, yes," I retorted. "I feel ever so much better now!"

And then, because I feared I would break down in tears at any moment, I whirled away from him and fled down the hallway to my room, where I flung myself down on the bed and wept as though my life had ended.

In my mind, it had.

CHAPTER 11

Dutiful wife that I was, I presented myself at the kitchen of Lord Sorthannic's castle promptly at seven o'clock the next morning. I wore the plainer of my two linen gowns, and had braided my hair out of the way and covered it with a white linen kerchief—which I was forced to borrow from Lynnis, for I had nothing like that in my possession.

A woman who appeared to be some ten years or so older than myself met me at the back door there and told me her name was Nerys. "I will take you to Brynna, the cook," she told me as she ushered me inside and through what appeared to be a large pantry, although it was bigger than the cottage where I now dwelt. Shelves on every side were filled with all manner of spices and preserves in jars, while stacked on the floor were sacks of flour and meal and potatoes. However, I did not have time to take more than a quick glance around, for Nerys kept up a brisk pace, one that did not encourage dawdling. Was this what I could expect of my days here?

Out in the kitchen itself, an enormous fire roared in the hearth set into one wall, while a round, red-cheeked woman was issuing commands to the two young women who stood at a large table in the center of the room. Piled around them was an assortment of vegetables, all of which were being chopped into precise one-inch chunks.

"She's here, mistress," Nerys said, and the round woman turned toward me. From the way her brows drew together and her lips pursed, I sensed that she was not overly impressed by my appearance.

"So you're Marenna?" the woman, who must be Brynna, inquired.

"Yes, mistress," I replied, and sketched a quick curtsey. Of course I had been trained to do so in a far more graceful manner, but I did not think that a cook merited quite the same courtesy as a duke, or an earl.

"How much experience do you have?"

If I confessed how new I was to all of this, I

rather doubted she would be impressed. Keeping my tone even, I said, "Perhaps not as much as the young woman I am replacing, but I am a quick learner, and my fingers are deft enough."

"Hmph." Brynna glanced over at the two girls who were chopping vegetables. "Alyse, check on the bread and see if it is rising properly."

"Yes, mistress," Alyse responded, and set down her knife before hurrying over to another table, where it seemed that several loaves of bread had been covered with muslin to protect them during the rising process.

"You," Brynna said, turning her attention back to me. "Go ahead and finish chopping those vegetables—but do not put them in the bowl. I want to inspect your work before I allow it to be part of his Grace's luncheon."

Her brusque tone made my heart sink that much further. How in the world was I supposed to endure this sort of treatment for months on end? My soul quailed at the very thought of it. But I also could not bear the thought of being sent away from the little cottage that was now my home, and so I knew I needed to do what I must to succeed here, no matter how I was spoken to, or what kinds of menial tasks I was given to perform.

I went and picked up the knife that Alyse had

discarded, and set to work. It was already clear to me that Brynna expected this task to be performed with precision, and so I did my very best to cut the potatoes and turnips and carrots into precise squares, as though somehow Lord Sorthannic's meal would be ruined if he was forced to eat food that wasn't completely symmetrical.

Brynna watched me for a moment, graying brows pulled together, her entire plump form seeming to radiate disapproval. "Is that the fastest you are able to work? I daresay those vegetables might be ready for tomorrow's supper, at the rate you are going."

My first instinct was to snap back at her, but somehow I managed to keep my tongue in check. I was doing this for Corin, and for our future together. I thought of how stiff and disapproving he had been the night before. I had not liked that, no, not at all. No, I wanted him to be proud of me—and I also wanted him to take me in his arms and hold me, to feel the warmth of his body and taste his lips once more.

"Not much to say for yourself?"

Once again I made myself remain quiet, although I pulled in a breath and had to count to five before I trusted myself to make a civil reply. "I am sorry, mistress. I will try to work more quickly. My husband did not require this kind of precision when I was preparing his meals."

She sniffed. "No, I suppose he wouldn't. However, this food is being set before the Duke of Marric's Rest, and so it must be perfect in every way."

"Yes, mistress." I bent my head over the table and tried to go a little faster, enough to prove that I was doing my best.

Another sniff, but this time she walked away and went over to inspect the bread, after which she told Alyse that it was rising well enough, and so she needed to go into the larder and churn a batch of fresh butter. The girl disappeared promptly, telling me that she was all too glad to be out of the cook's presence, even if it meant tiring herself while coaxing butter from a churn full of buttermilk.

I continued to chop away, every once in a while shooting surreptitious glances at the mound of vegetables set off to one side, and wondering how on earth one man could require so much food. To be honest, I did not know that much about Lord Sorthannic's household. He was unmarried and had no children. His family was far away—his mother and father in South Eredor, his sister married to the ruler of North

Eredor. As far as I had been able to tell, his was quite the solitary existence.

But perhaps he was expecting guests. I had heard he was great good friends with Duke Senric, who was lately married to Gabrinne, the daughter of the Earl of Kelsir. Perhaps the duke and his bride were coming to stay for a time. I recalled how Corin had said Lord Sorthannic would be hosting a harvest ball, but that was still almost a week away. Then again, I had only a very hazy idea of how far in advance food would be prepared for such a momentous event. It was entirely possible that we were already working on such fare. But no, Brynna had said this was all for his Grace's luncheon.

I chopped away, frowning slightly as I attempted to ponder the situation. At the same time, I wondered what Corin might be up to at this particular moment. From what I'd been able to tell, this was a delicate time for the grapes, and the crush needed to be watched over carefully to make sure it would be ready to be filtered and moved into barrels at the proper time. Perhaps my husband was with Master Brinsell, inspecting the vats and preparing for the transfer. After the hard work he had put in since coming to the estate, a more leisurely day would be a happy change of pace.

As for myself, well, at least it seemed as if Brynna had other matters to occupy her attention, for a moment later she disappeared into the pantry/storeroom, and we kitchen maids were left blissfully alone. I stole a quick glance from under my lashes at the other girl chopping vegetables, whose name I still did not know. However, it appeared that she was in no mood to steal a few words now that the cook was away, for although her eyes met mine for a few seconds, she quickly looked back down at her work, seeming to indicate that she would not allow herself to talk while she toiled away, even when left alone.

Very well. I certainly had no desire to cause any problems, or to get someone I did not even know in trouble, merely because talking might help to pass the time. And a good thing, too, for a moment later, Brynna reappeared, this time carrying a dizzying amount of spices and other items from the storerooms. She busied herself at the other end of the table, grating and grinding and chopping, assembling what looked to me like an astonishing array of ingredients. What it was all for, I couldn't begin to guess, but I would be the first to admit that my knowledge of cookery and complicated dishes was not very extensive. Lynnis had showed me how to make certain simple meals, of course. Then again, simply recalling all the food served in the castle where I had grown up told me that there was an entire world of which I knew very little.

However, I was pleased by Brynna's preoccupation, for it meant that she did not have as much time to criticize what I was doing. I startled slightly when the other kitchen girl came over and scooped up everything I had chopped so far and put it in a bowl, but I supposed that was something of a good sign, for it meant that what I had prepared had apparently passed muster.

I could not help but watch in some curiosity, however, as a man wearing the household's black and silver livery appeared a few minutes later, and went to whisper something to Brynna. Immediately she left off from chopping her herbs and went to the table where the bread was rising. In another basket sitting there was a batch of new, fresh rolls. Even from where I stood, I could smell their warm aroma, and my stomach growled. Luckily, no one seemed to notice, but the reaction served to remind me that I had had only a bit of bread and some tea before setting out this morning. Would we have any luncheon here? Would I be allowed to go home to eat? Or would I have to slave away all day with barely any food in my belly?

If I had been a bit braver, I might have tried to ask. As it was, I watched as Brynna went to a huge cupboard that covered most of one wall, and retrieved a silver platter and a fine plate, also silver. Alyse reappeared with a pretty little pat of butter on a matching silver plate, and set it down on the platter Brynna had just gotten from the cupboard. Next came two of the rolls. At the same time, the footman went to a kettle that had been hanging over the stove and poured some hot water into a little silver pot that had been sitting out on the counter next to the fireplace. The pot went on the platter, all was arranged in a combination pleasing to the eye, and he went back out, the door swinging shut behind him.

I raised an eyebrow at Brynna. To my relief, she did not reprimand me for my impertinence, but only said, "His lordship's breakfast. He does not care to eat much in the morning, but will have his bread and tea. That is why his luncheon must be so substantial."

"I see," I replied. "Substantial" was all very well and good, but at the moment it seemed as if we were preparing enough food for at least ten people.

However, as the morning wore on, and the chopped vegetables were added to the base Brynna had created with all her herbs and spices and a goodly amount of wine, along with some venison that she cut into cubes herself, I learned that the savory stew we had all helped to create was not intended merely for Lord Sorthannic, but for Master Brinsell as well, and my own Corin, and the other men who were working in the cellars with him.

Not only that, but each of us in the kitchen was given a good portion of the stew as well, and a slice of bread with butter. The food was delicious, allaying my fears from earlier that I was to be made to starve all day.

And it seemed that, unless he had guests visiting, the duke consumed his biggest meal in the middle of the day. Brynna watched over Alyse and me as we prepared a pigeon pie for his Grace's dinner—although the cook made the pastry shell herself—but I was sent home in the late afternoon after that task was done, for I would not be needed again until the morning.

Which meant I had time to prepare something for Corin and myself. By that point I was heartily sick of looking at the interior of a kitchen, even if it happened to be my own, but I needed to come up with something. Luckily, I had eggs and cheese and bread, and so I layered them all together in a pan, and set them to bake over the fire. Combined with some figs Lynnis had brought over the day before, the dish would make a nice light meal, which sounded very well to me, since I had eaten so heartily in the middle of the day.

When Corin came home, he appeared relieved that I was not weeping in my room again, or at the very least sulking over my first day of being a kitchen drudge in his lordship's castle. Indeed, I told him that it had all gone very well, and I was not all that wearied, and I hoped he would enjoy his dinner.

He sat at the table and smiled at me, and said, "This all looks very good, Marenna, and was more than I expected, frankly. So the work was not so awful after all?"

"Well, Brynna, the cook, can be rather formidable when she wants. But we ate very well, and because his Grace is not entertaining any guests at the moment, there was no reason for me to stay late and help cook for a multitude. So if my days in the castle follow that particular pattern, I think I should survive this fairly well."

Corin nodded, but I watched as his smile faded. He said, "That holds true for now, but I believe the duke is expecting a large number of guests for his harvest ball, which is now only five days hence."

The hopeful feeling I had been holding

within me as I walked home from the castle began to ebb, but I said stoutly, "I suppose that is true, but even so, that will only be for a few days while his guests are still here. As soon as they have all gone home, things will return to normal, and, as far as I can tell, 'normal' is very easy to manage."

"I am glad you see it that way." He ate a few bites of his baked bread and cheese, and nodded in approval. "This is very tasty. Where did you learn to make such a thing?"

"Oh, Lynnis told me. She said it is good for those times when you don't have other ingredients on hand, or simply haven't the time to make something more complicated."

"Clever...and practical." Another bite, and then he set down his fork. "And perhaps you will also begin to pick up a few tips and tricks by working in Brynna's kitchen."

"I hope so," I said honestly, for the thought had passed through my mind that I could learn from my work in the castle and so be able to offer more dishes to set on the table at home. "However, I could not see all that Brynna was doing today as she prepared that venison stew, and at any rate, she included so many complicated herbs and spices that I am sure we could never afford to stock them all here."

"Perhaps. We may be able to do with less." He paused before adding, "And I have not spent all that much of those fifty gold crowns your father gave me. Once the harvest ball is over, we might see about taking a short trip to Elmcroft to do some shopping. At the very least, we should get you some new shoes."

Oh, yes, that was a very good idea. Because the weather had remained fine, and I had not been doing anything too strenuous, my poor battered slippers were limping along, mostly because Lynnis had showed me how to slide a piece of thin leather inside them to help strengthen the worn-out soles. However, I could already tell that walking back and forth from my cottage to the castle every day was only going to subject them to more wear and tear, and if it should rain—well, I really did not want to contemplate what a good downpour and some mud might do to those slippers.

"That sounds wonderful," I said. "A day away —I think I would like that very much."

"Then let us plan for it." His expression grew quite serious. "I am very proud of you, Marenna, for doing so well today, even though I know you dreaded having to go to the castle and work. But I hope you see now that it is not quite as terrible as you imagined."

"No, it was not." I paused, wishing to gather my thoughts on the subject. At first Brynna had quite intimidated me, but it seemed obvious enough that if I took care as I went about my duties, and was quiet and meek, then we should get on well enough. Yes, I would be the first to admit that "meek" was not a word generally used to describe me, but if I had learned nothing else over the past week, it was that I needed to choose my battles. Squabbling with the cook because she had said something that offended my pride would gain me nothing and very likely could cause me to be dismissed. I couldn't risk such an outcome, simply because of wounded vanity. "It could have been far, far worse. I think I can manage well enough, especially if I remind myself that it is not permanent."

Corin did not respond, beyond inclining his head slightly and returning to the food which still remained on his plate. What that response meant, I was not sure. He had told me that he thought I would only have to work through the winter, but what if Master Brinsell had said something to disabuse him of that notion?

Well, then, I told myself, *you will just have to do something that ensures Brynna will not want you to work there. Something that is no fault of your own.*

Easier said than done. But then I recalled how the girl who had held my post previously left because she had just given birth to her first child. I supposed I could use the same excuse, except that would mean....

It would mean you could not avoid sharing your husband's bed any longer, I thought. *So you will have to decide what is more fearsome to you —spending the rest of this autumn and all of the winter working in Lord Sorthannic's kitchen, or giving yourself to the man who married you.*

Some might say that was an easy enough choice. After all, I had felt myself so very close the other night. But what if Corin rebuffed me again? I was not sure I could bear further rejection, even though I must have also tried his patience.

And then I realized I could not coldly lie with him, just to escape my duties. I did not want it to be that way between us. I had come to care for him—indeed, as I pretended to be preoccupied with finishing the rest of the food on my plate, but instead watched him through my eyelashes, I realized how much I cared, how I wanted him to kiss me and make me his.

"Corin," I began, then stopped, for I was not quite sure how I could continue. Every combination of words I put together in my mind sounded dreadful, no matter how much I tried to shift them around into something that made sense.

He looked up from his own plate, expression quizzical. "What is it, Marenna?"

"I—" I pulled in a breath, then said quickly, "I no longer wish to sleep in the second bedroom."

His dark eyes flared with surprise, but then he shook his head. When he spoke, his tone was flat. "You are tired. You don't know what you are asking."

"I *do* know!" I flung at him, both angry at my husband for his intransigence and embarrassed at myself for being so bold. "Lynnis explained it all to me, so I do know very well. I'm—I'm not afraid any longer. It is foolish for us to be married and yet live as chastely as a brother and sister. Or," I added, as that familiar shuttered look took over his features, the one I hated so much, "is it that you don't find me as tempting as you once thought you did? Perhaps it was one thing to have moonlight and wine and dancing to enhance my charms, but when you see me now as a maidservant, my hands already turning rough with work, my clothing plain and drab and stained, you begin to have second thoughts."

"That is not it at all," he said. His tone was even enough, but a shadow of anguish remained in his eyes. "I can't—I cannot explain everything to you right now. But please believe me when I tell you that there is a reason why I choose to wait."

"For how long?" I asked. Tears began to burn in my eyes. I ignored them, however, and went on without waiting for his answer. "A few days ago, I would have said you could not wait to make me yours. And now you are telling me to be patient, that there is a reason to delay even further?"

"Yes, that is precisely what I am telling you." He rubbed at his chin, at the dark stubble that had begun to show there. In my former life, I would have said that stubble was a sign of his lowly origins, of his not caring enough to groom himself properly, but now I thought it only enhanced his darkly handsome looks. "Marenna, I do nothing without a reason. This may seem strange and incomprehensible to you now, but very soon, you will understand."

"If you say so." Because both our plates had been scraped clean, I got up from my seat and stacked them on top of one another, then stalked off to the kitchen. I hoped that Corin would follow me, but as I set the plates down on the counter and placed the kettle over the fire to heat the water so I might wash them, I realized I was still quite alone, that he had left me to my own devices.

More than ever, I wanted to weep, but I choked the tears back and continued with my task, determined to leave a clean kitchen behind. I could not allow myself the luxury of ignoring the dirty dishes until the following morning, for I would have to be up early and at work in the castle.

So there was a reason for all this? I could only hope my husband would reveal it to me soon, before the rift between us had widened so much that there was no longer any chance of repairing it.

CHAPTER 12

I WISH I COULD SAY THAT MATTERS IMPROVED between us after that squabble, but unfortunately, they did not. My days were spent working in the duke's kitchen, while Corin was occupied in the cellars, and we did not have much of a chance to repair our relations. Oh, we were polite to one another, but we might as well have been strangers, all of the rapport that had begun to grow between us now gone as if it had never been. It was as if my husband had erected an invisible barrier between us, one he wished to keep in place for reasons known only to him.

If the gods were kind, I would have at least had the opportunity to share my troubles with Lynnis and ask for her guidance, but it seemed those same gods who delighted in making my own existence a miserable one had chosen to smile down upon her, for she was now confined to her bed with the nausea of early pregnancy. Hal passed on the good news to Corin, who at least had the courtesy to tell me. As happy as I was for Lynnis, I could not help but experience a flash of disappointment. Who else could I turn to, when things had gone so wrong between my husband and myself? I had not made friends with any of the other women in the settlement, for none of them were close to my age, and all of them were preoccupied with their children and their households. And soon Lynnis would be just as preoccupied.

Whereas I....

These gloomy thoughts crowded my mind as I walked home from my third day working in the kitchens of Lord Sorthannic's castle. I supposed I should be happy that I had survived another shift under Brynna's watchful eye, but at the moment, I could not help but feel sorry for myself.

The weather was certainly not cooperating, either, for midway through my walk a cold, thin rain began to fall. At least I was not completely unprepared, for the day had been chilly enough when I set out in the morning that I had wrapped a woolen shawl around my shoulders. However, the shawl did nothing to protect my feet in their worn slippers. I was still far from home when I felt the wet begin to seep through, soaking my already icy toes.

It will be all right, I told myself as I tried to ignore the uncomfortable squelching while I walked. *When you get home, you will stir up the kitchen fire and set your shoes by the hearth to dry. Why, after you change out these stockings for some fresh ones, you will not even be able to tell that you got soaked coming home.*

That all sounded very brave in my mind. However, with each pace my heart seemed to sink a little lower, and at some point tears began to trail down my cheeks, mixing with the stinging rain. Not that there was anyone around to see; the weather appeared to have driven everyone indoors, and I saw none of the usual activities of children playing in the square, or women taking down their laundry after letting it dry on the line all day. No, any laundry must have been whisked inside at the first sight of rain, and was probably now doing its best to dry next to everyone's kitchen hearths.

Head bowed, I hurried inside, then took off my damp shawl and draped it over the back of one of the kitchen chairs. No sign of Corin, but his absence did not surprise me too much, as he tended to come home at least an hour after I did, if not more.

I had carefully stoked the kitchen fire before I left that morning, but it seemed my efforts had been in vain, for the hearth was as cold and grey as the day outside. After wiping my cheeks, I went to get the box of matches and some fresh wood. Thank goodness we had a decent supply in the basket in the corner, for it really would have been too much to go back outside in the rain and wrestle with wet logs, not to mention sending all manner of smoke into the kitchen... even if I had somehow managed to start a fire at all.

But since the logs I used were dry, the fire leapt up soon enough, sending its welcome warmth into the kitchen. With a sigh of relief, I bent down and removed my slippers, then turned them over to inspect their soles. As I had feared, both of the shoes sported new holes, down near the toes on the right slipper and on the heel of the left slipper. The pieces of leather Lynnis had given me to help line them were also starting to wear through. Perhaps I could try patching them, but I did not think such clumsy repairs would last for very long—if I even could find a needle sturdy enough to pierce the battered kid.

My eyes stung again, and I blinked. Standing

here and weeping would do me no good, not when I needed to get supper started. Luckily, Hal had brought over a pair of rabbits the evening before, bounty from a particularly successful hunt. I had tried to protest that we could not accept such a gift, but he had only smiled and said he could not allow me to return the game meat he had given us.

So I had rabbits to roast over the fire—Hal had taken pity on me, and presented them to me already skinned and ready to be cooked—and new potatoes, and field greens to make a salad. It would be a fine meal, although I feared even such a repast would not be enough to make Corin soften toward me.

More than once my maid Sendra had told me that men did not like a forward woman. To be fair, at the time I had not been entirely clear as to what she had meant by the word "forward," but now I could see what she had intended with her advice. For when I had spoken the truth of my heart, had not tried to hide my feelings from Corin, he had turned away from me. It seemed he had wanted me to be coy, and shy, and allow him to do the pursuing. I was neither coy nor shy, but I thought I would make the attempt, if by doing so I might soften his heart.

For as much as I wanted to tell myself I did

not care, that I *should* not care what a lowly farm worker might think of me, I knew that was a lie. My heart had opened to Corin in a way I had not thought possible. As cool as he had been these past few days, I knew his behavior did not reflect his true self. No, he was warm and caring, and had done a great deal for me. If I were a user of magic, I would have fashioned a spell to send myself back in time and fix whatever had gone amiss between us that night, so we would not now be estranged.

Alas, I had no such powers, and not many useful skills, either. I was learning—albeit more slowly than I would have liked—but being talented enough not to burn one's toast in the morning was not quite the sort of ability required to heal the rift that had opened between my husband and myself.

Once I had set a pot of water to boil over the fire, so I might start the potatoes after the water had heated enough, I went into my bedroom and got out a fresh pair of stockings, and removed the damp ones I currently wore. They, too, had begun to develop holes, and upon seeing that damage, I could not help but let out an exasperated sigh. Yes, darning stockings did lie within my range of skills, but finding the time to perform such repairs was an entirely different proposition. And I knew I did not have the proper needle and thread for such a task, since I had left them at Lynnis' cottage several days earlier, when I had been showing her how to repair her husband's socks. I would have to ask to get them back from her, and hope that I was not disturbing her too much by going over to her cottage and making such a request.

I had just finished tying off the garters for my clean pair of stockings when I heard a knock at the door. Puzzled, I left my room and went to answer it, wondering who would be making a call at such an hour, and in such weather. Certainly Corin would not knock, and it seemed that Lynnis had been confined to her bed for the foreseeable future. But perhaps one of the other women in the settlement had need of a cup of flour or some other necessary ingredient, having miscalculated what she had on hand to follow a recipe.

When I opened the door, however, my heart seemed to freeze in my chest. For there was the last person I had expected to see—my father, draped in an elegant black cloak, a jaunty be-feathered felt hat protecting his head from the rain, although the crimson feather in that hat was now beginning to droop from the damp.

At first I could only stare at him, sure that my

mind must have manufactured this apparition. How else could he be here? But then his dark eyes fastened on mine, and he tilted his head and said, "Will you not let me in, daughter?"

"Oh—oh, yes, of course," I replied, then held the door open a little wider so he might come inside. "Let me take your cloak and hat."

"Thank you." He removed the garments in question and held them out to me, and I hurried over to hang them from the rack in one corner. The whole time, his gaze was moving about the room, no doubt taking in the plain furnishings, the bare walls.

I had prided myself on keeping the cottage clean and neat, but now I could only see my current home through his eyes, noting the smudge of damp on one wall, the scuffs and scrapes on the table and chairs. A far cry from the sumptuous carved furniture of my former home, the tapestries on the walls, the rich rugs of Keshiaari weave that covered the floors. Indeed, I could not help but be struck by the splendor of my father's garments, the embroidered wool of his doublet, the fine linen of the shirt he wore underneath, the glint of the ruby in the heavy gold ring he wore. After so much time spent among people who dressed simply out of necessity, the ostentation of my father's clothing was almost jarring.

His gaze traveled to the stockinged feet peeping out from under my plain brown skirt, and he frowned.

"My shoes were damp after the walk home," I explained. "They are drying by the fire. But please, sit down, Father." I gestured toward one of the chairs at the table, the only seat I could offer him.

"'Walk home'?" he repeated, his frown deepening. "Why would you be any place but here, especially in this weather?"

"Oh, I—" It seemed too dreadful to try to explain to him that I had been working in the castle's kitchen, and so I said quickly, "I went to check on my neighbor, who is with child. But Father—what are you doing here?"

He hesitated and would not look directly at me. At last he let out a heavy breath, shaking his head. "My treatment of you has been weighing on me, Marenna. At last I realized I could bear it no more, and knew I must come here to beg your forgiveness...and ask you to come home with me."

For a moment, I could not quite comprehend what he had just told me. Home? But was this not my home? "I...I am not sure I understand," I said.

"What I did to you, my dear—it was wrong. Wrong, and terrible. In the heat of the moment, I could only think of teaching you a lesson. But as the days wore on, and I thought more of what I had done, I knew that I must try to come to you and make it right." My father glanced around the room as though looking for someone, even when it should have been clear enough that we were alone in the cottage. It certainly was not large enough to conceal other occupants. "Where is your husband?"

"Still working at the castle," I replied. "His duties often keep him there somewhat late. Indeed, he is quite knowledgeable about wine and has already been given the post of under-overseer. I think that Master Brinsell has come to quite rely on him."

"Master Brinsell?"

"He is the overseer of the fields and also the master of the cellar. They produce some very fine wines here on the estate." Although I tried my best to sound neutral, I could not quite prevent a note of pride from creeping into my voice. I wanted my father to know that Corin was not a common laborer, but a man possessed of valuable knowledge, someone who was looked upon as a welcome addition to Lord Sorthannic's household.

My father made an offhand wave, as if impatient with my explanation. "Yes, I know of the wines of Marric's Rest—we have enjoyed them on more than one occasion at our own table. And I suppose it is good to know that Master Blackstone has more to offer than just a handsome face and a pleasant manner. However, you deserve much more than merely being the wife of an estate's under-overseer. You deserve someone splendid, a husband who can give you the sort of life you were born to."

It was on the tip of my tongue to tell him that perhaps he should have kept such considerations in mind before he sent me off to be the wife of a stranger, but somehow I managed to keep silent. After all, his expression now was one of utter contrition. He had come here to make things right, and I knew I must give him some credit for that.

And truly, I knew he could—if I allowed him to. Although annulments were very uncommon things in Sirlende, they did happen from time to time, and tended to be the subject of scandalized, whispered conversations at balls and supper parties. When I had overheard some of those conversations, the finer points had eluded me, for back then I did not yet possess intimate knowledge of what a proper marriage was supposed to be. Now, though, I understood that I would be granted an annulment, if my father and I went to Iselfex to plead my case. I was not Corin's wife in any true sense of the word. Also, my father's influence and wealth would be squarely on my side. If I wished, I could be a free woman within a very short period of time.

Contemplating such a possibility, however, only stirred a strange reluctance within me. I realized I did not wish to be free, that my feelings for Corin were not such that I could easily ignore them. In a perfect world, I would wish to have him and the luxurious life I had previously enjoyed, but if forced to make a choice, I knew I would rather remain with him in this humble cottage than go back to a life of ease that excluded him. Our current coolness was a temporary thing, no more. Once we had cleared up whatever might have caused that misunderstanding, we could truly be together. I was sure of it.

My father was watching me closely, his greying dark brows pulled together. No doubt he was attempting to puzzle out why I would remain silent for so long. After all, the daughter who had left his estate only a little more than a week earlier would have jumped at the chance to abandon this life of poverty, to return to her world of balls and coaches and fine gowns, and breakfast in bed brought to her by one of the chambermaids.

The thought of those lovely breakfast trays, with tea and cinnamon buns and eggs and bacon, did make me a bit wistful. But I realized then that I would rather have Corin in my bed than any number of breakfast trays. It was quite the bold thought, especially with my father sitting only a few feet away from me. I could not deny the truth of my heart, though. In that moment, I knew I would much rather be the wife of Corin Blackstone, under-overseer, than the spoiled daughter of Silverhold Hall.

"I am not so sure it is a matter of what I deserve," I said slowly, attempting to choose my words with care, for I did not want to offend my father, who clearly had put aside his own pride to journey to Marric's Rest and plead for me to come home. "It is more that being here with Corin has taught me something more of what the world has to offer. There can be a simple beauty in this kind of life, one I didn't even realize existed before now. He has been very kind and has treated me well. Should I be a coward and run away, simply because this is not the life I was born to?"

"You are not a coward," my father protested. "It is not as though you came to me and begged for release from this marriage I thrust upon you. From what I have been able to see of you today, you have borne up under these hardships with far more grace than most might have expected."

"Indeed?" I was not sure whether to be amused or annoyed by this pronouncement. Had my father so little faith in my strength of character, my resilience? But then, I supposed I had not given much indication of strength or resilience in the past, not when I had been known to lose my temper over something so silly as the wrong color of ribbons used to tie back my hair. "Well, I am glad to know that I have exceeded your expectations, Father. However, you know I cannot leave. No, rather, I *will* not leave. I will not do that to Corin, to make him be the man whose wife left him because she did not care enough to struggle her way through a new kind of life."

For a long moment, my father said nothing. Indeed, from the way he stared at me, it seemed that he was attempting to determine whether I was in fact the same daughter who had left her childhood home only a short week and a half earlier. I could not precisely fault him for thinking such a thing, for the Marenna I had been a scant ten days ago would not have uttered such words. Corin had helped to wreak such a change in me, and I had to thank him for that.

"Can it be that you do truly care for him?"

"Yes," I said stoutly, hoping that the firmness in my voice would help to convince him of my sincerity. "I do...very much. You might have thought that you were teaching me a lesson, Father, or perhaps you believed that you had not given very much thought to the man who would be the agent of such a teaching exercise. However, it seems your fatherly instincts won out, for I do believe that if someone had presented himself who was not worthy in your eyes, you would not have sent me away with him. Now I cannot think of being with anyone but Corin, which means he has turned out to be the choice of my heart, even if it did not seem that way in the beginning."

"I am...surprised," my father managed in response to my statement, which was only the truth. He still wore an expression of astonishment, as though his mind and heart still could not quite comprehend the veracity of what I had told him.

I smiled. "I am also surprised...at myself, at what my heart has been trying to tell me for the past few days. I must thank you, Father, for perhaps I needed you to come here and try to convince me to leave in order for me to know the truth of my feelings. Do not trouble yourself over me, because I know I am where I am supposed to be. However," I added with a chuckle, "if you could perhaps send me a sturdy pair of shoes, I would most appreciate it. My slippers are nearly in tatters, and I know they cannot survive the winter."

He shook his head, another frown touching his brow. "Are your straits so dire that your husband cannot provide you with the proper shoes?"

"Oh, no," I replied at once. "We can afford it, but we are so busy right now that finding the time to go to Elmcroft and have a new pair made is quite out of the question. I left many pairs of shoes behind, so it should be simple enough to have Sendra package up some of them and send them to me."

"I will see to it," my father said. I heard the resignation in his tone, as though he was agreeing to this only because he knew he could say nothing to dissuade me from my course. At least by sending me some shoes, he could tell himself that he had done what he could to help me.

"Thank you, Father."

He rose from his chair then and extended a hand to me. I took it, watched as he wrapped his fingers around mine and gave them a gentle squeeze before letting go. His skin felt very soft compared to Corin's work-hardened touch.

But then, my father had never done anything more strenuous than follow the hounds on the hunt. I did not know why I should be expecting to feel the calluses of a laboring man.

A few steps toward the door, and then he turned and stared down at me, his expression pleading. "You are sure of this, Marenna? Absolutely sure? I know that no one will think the less of you if you come away with me now."

"*I* will think less of me," I responded. "And that is enough for me to know that I have made the right choice. I could not do such a thing to Corin. He does not deserve such treatment."

My father nodded, and said, "He is a lucky man. I hope he knows that he has inspired such devotion."

Did he know? I thought I had made my own feelings on the subject quite clear, but perhaps that was part of the problem. Perhaps Corin had spurned me because he thought I was toying with him in some way.

Well, I would simply have to find some way to disabuse him of that notion.

"He knows," I said, my tone firm.

"Well, then." A pause, and my father added, "May the gods smile on you, Marenna."

"And on you, Father," I replied.

He smiled then, but it was a rueful smile, as though he thought I was the one far more in need of the gods' favor than he. However, he did not respond, but settled his hat more firmly on his head and drew his cloak around him, then headed out into the rainy night.

I shut the door behind him and prayed I had made the right choice.

CHAPTER 13

OVER THE COURSE OF THE NEXT FEW DAYS, I FELT as though my judgment was being sorely tested, for even as preparations for the upcoming harvest ball at the castle grew to a fever pitch, it seemed that Corin became more and more distant and distracted, less inclined to speak with me or even comfort me with a smile. No, whatever weighed on his mind, clearly it was not something he wished to share with me.

Unsure as to what I should do, I withdrew as well. I only made perfunctory inquiries about his day when he came home in the evening and delivered the most desultory of remarks about the weather in the morning before he departed. Yes, because I had vowed to be a good wife to him, I made sure that meals were prepared and the cottage kept as clean as I could manage, what with most of my day spent in the castle's kitchen, but I would not go any further than that. Certainly I did not bother to renew my pursuit of him. It seemed I was now doubly a servant, both at the castle and in the cottage that was now my home. Even so, I would not give Corin the satisfaction of knowing how disappointed I was by the current state of affairs.

The only bright note was that Lynnis appeared to have gotten over the worst of her sickness, and she sent word that she wanted to speak with me. My spare time was limited in the extreme, but my desire to see her was even greater than my need to sweep the cottage before dinner, and so I hurried over to her house— modest and plain, but still finer than mine—glad that Corin should not be home for another hour or so.

She seemed well enough that she was able to sit up, but I noted that she looked rather pale, the lively glow gone from her cheeks. However, it seemed churlish to remark upon such a detail, especially since her current appearance was a result of the blessing for which she'd waited so long. Instead, I pulled up a chair and sat down across from her by the hearth. It did feel good to sit and rest my aching feet, to enjoy the warmth of a fire I hadn't had to build myself.

Apparently, being confined to her bed for a few days hadn't done much to mar her powers of observation. One eyebrow lifted, and she looked me up and down, then shook her head. "You do not seem to be particularly blooming of late, Mistress Blackstone."

I might have said the same of her, except that I had already made a vow to myself not to comment on her wan looks. However, it seemed she must have read my thoughts, because she chuckled and continued,

"Oh, I know I am not the perfect picture of health at the moment, either. But this will pass, and I am certain that in no time I will be as rosy and blooming as any woman who has carried a child." Her smile faded slightly, and she cocked a head at me. "So, Marenna, tell me what is amiss. We are long overdue for a chat."

The same thought had passed through my head many times already, but now that I faced my friend, I was not sure how much I should tell her. She already had enough to occupy her mind. And really, it was not as though I had anything terribly earth-shaking to confide in her. I could not even say that Corin and I had quarreled. Our current problem appeared to be indifference, not anger.

I lifted my shoulders. "Oh, I suppose it is only that all the preparations at the castle have begun to wear on me. Perhaps it is a good thing that so many dishes—or at least the components required for them—can be prepared in advance, but it does seem to make the whole ordeal last much longer than it should."

Her gaze was sympathetic. "Yes, the duke's harvest ball is quite the event of the year in this part of the world. Of course I have never attended, but I've heard the stories. Also, his Grace is kind enough to send some of the leftover food down here to the settlement the day after the party, so we all get a chance to taste the delicacies that the noble lords and ladies dined on the evening before."

Did that mean I would have an opportunity to consume some of the very food which was currently making my life such a nightmare? For some reason, that notion seemed to make the whole ordeal even worse. After putting so much effort into them, I found I didn't have much appetite for all those refined dishes.

"How very noble of him," I remarked. "It is too bad his Grace's nobility doesn't extend toward hiring extra help, rather than making those already on his household staff have to shoulder far too large a burden."

Rather than the sympathetic noises I had expected, Lynnis only tilted her head at me and shot a curious glance in my direction. "But it is *all* part of their duties. They know the harvest ball is coming, and plan for it accordingly." Apparently, I did not look too impressed by this line of reasoning, for she then leaned over and patted my hand. "It seems hard because it is all very new to you. I imagine that next year you will not think it any great ordeal."

At once I widened my eyes at her and gave a shake of my head. "Oh, no, there will not be a 'next year.' Corin assured me that this work in the kitchen is only temporary. Once he is firmly established here as the under-overseer, there will be no need for me to work at the castle at all."

Judging by my friend's dubious expression, it seemed that she did not quite believe this fairy story. However, she also did not appear inclined to argue, thank the gods, for she gave a very small lift of her shoulders and said, "Ah, well, if that is the case, I suppose you can look on this one time as a little adventure you once had, and nothing more. But I am sorry that it has turned out to be such a burden."

Her words led me to think that she had never

had to shoulder such a burden herself, for Hal's contributions to the estate were enough to support the two of them. That realization made me frown inwardly, however. As far as I could tell, Lynnis' husband had far fewer skills than Corin, and yet the two of them seemed to manage well enough on what Hal earned as a simple laborer. But then, he and Lynnis had both been born here at Marric's Rest, had spent their entire lives on the estate. Perhaps Lord Sorthannic thought their history merited them more consideration than a pair of strangers who had appeared here out of nowhere, asking for work. Corin—and I by extension as his wife— must needs toil much harder to prove our worth.

"It will be over in a few days," I said. For indeed, I knew that to only be the truth. However much I might find myself suffering now, this chaos could not last forever. By the day after tomorrow, matters should have returned to normal, or at least as normal as they could be, with such coolness existing between my husband and myself.

"Precisely," Lynnis replied with a smile. Her hand moved to her belly, which still appeared quite flat to me. "Whereas I have many more months to go."

"Ah, but the child is something you have long

hoped and wished for. I cannot say the same thing about my time in the kitchens of Lord Sorthannic's castle!"

In response to that remark, she could only laugh aloud and say, "Well, that much is true. And Tharis brought over some peppermint tea, which has done a great deal to calm my stomach. I do not think it can do much to help you with your kitchen work, unfortunately!"

No, there was not a tea which existed that could soothe my current ills. Only the passage of time would cure my troubles...and perhaps not even then, if Corin and I could not find a way to smooth away the bumps that had surfaced over the past few days.

"No, probably not," I said. "But I am glad that you have found something to help you feel better, and doubly glad that the gods have chosen to smile upon you. When will the babe make his appearance in the world?"

"Sometime in late spring, I think. That is a piece of good luck for me, for I will not have the burden of carrying a child in the heat of the summer. Why, Nelys had her youngest at the height of August, and she looked as though she might faint at any moment toward the end."

I could only imagine how difficult that must be. Of course Sirlende did not have the brutal summers of Keshiaar, where I had heard the desert sands grew so hot the very air shimmered above them, but it could still be uncomfortably warm. Those drowsy summer days had often sent me to lie down in my room during the peak heat of the afternoon, clad only in a chemise, for even my lightest linen gowns had felt like too much of a burden. However, a woman of Lynnis' station—or Nelys'—did not have the luxury of taking such a rest. She must continue to work, whether or not she was heavy with child.

That might be my fate as well, except that right then I did not think I had much to fear in terms of carrying a child. At the moment, Corin seemed barely inclined to speak to me, let alone touch me in the way that would quicken a life within my womb.

"Yes, that is quite fortuitous," I said. "One might think you planned it that way."

"Oh, I am not that clever. Determined, yes, and my determination finally paid off. But I would never presume to say that I had planned for matters to turn out this way."

No, I supposed she had not. As I shifted in my chair, I realized that the view out the window had grown dim and dusky, the sun now set. I had spent longer here than I planned, and I knew I must hurry home, or dinner would be terribly late. Rising from my chair, I made a hasty apology to Lynnis, telling her I must go immediately.

She brushed away my apology and said, "I had not realized it was so late. Of course it is time for you to go home. I suppose I shall not see you tomorrow, but the day after you must come over and let me know all about the ball. I would love you to describe all the fine ladies to me."

That last thing I wanted was to be able to give a description of those "fine ladies," for that would mean I was in a position to see them in all their silken splendor. I did not wish for such a thing, no, quite the opposite. My most fervent desire was to be able to hide in the kitchen all evening, and never set foot outside its door.

However, I knew I could not tell Lynnis these things, for she would want to know why on earth I did not wish to catch a glimpse of Lord Sorthannic's guests. I could not tell her the truth; the story of my origins was not something I wanted bandied about the settlement. Perhaps one day I would feel comfortable with everyone knowing my true history, but I certainly was not about to make such revelations now. Besides, as uncharitable as the thought might be, I did not know for sure whether Lynnis was inclined to gossip, or whether I could trust her to keep all my secrets.

"I will do my best," I said, my voice noncommittal, and bent and squeezed her hand before I let myself out.

Unlike the evening when my father had so unexpectedly visited me, it was a fine night, with a warm yellow moon rising behind the hills to the east, now a fat gibbous shape only a few days away from full. No doubt Lord Sorthannic had timed his harvest ball to coincide with the bright moon. However, I could not tarry to revel in its splendor, for I was already terribly late. It was a good thing that all I had planned for dinner was cold chicken pie and some fruit compote.

When I entered the cottage, I saw that I was even later than I'd thought, for candles flickered on the table where Corin and I took our meals, and on the plain wood mantel above the hearth. My husband sat at the table, one of our stoneware goblets sitting in front of him.

"They had you working very late tonight," he said.

For a scant second I considered agreeing with him, letting him think that I had come home directly from the castle. But even with all the coolness between us, I still did not wish to lie to him. "Actually, I was at Lynnis' home," I replied.

"She was well enough to see me, and we had a little chat. I truly did not realize it was this late. I will get dinner out immediately."

"No need to rush." He tipped his head to one side and sent me a searching glance. "And no need to look so worried, my wife. I am not one of those boors who feels it is within his rights to beat his wife simply because dinner is a half hour late reaching the table."

"No, of course not," I said. Whatever might have caused the separation between us, it certainly was not because I feared Corin. Yes, I had heard that some men behaved in such a way toward their wives, but my husband was certainly not one of those brutish types. "But I am sure you are hungry...as am I."

I left the room then and went to the kitchen. It was the work of only a few short moments to cut slices of cold chicken pie—Corin's piece much larger than mine—and to add some spiced apple compote and pieces of bread to our plates. I hurried out to the table where my husband sat and set his plate in front of him.

"There you are," I said as I took my own plate and put it in front of my chair before sitting down.

"You do not wish for any wine?" he inquired,

clearly noting that I had neglected to bring out a goblet for myself.

"Oh," I faltered. Truly, I would have liked some wine, but at the same time, I did not wish to get up again. "No," I went on, "for I shall have a long day tomorrow, and I do not wish to tire myself today, which is what I fear a glass of wine would do to me."

Corin seemed to accept this explanation, for he shrugged and picked up his fork, then helped himself to a large mouthful of pie. I did the same, although I was not very hungry. Strange, because with all the running back and forth I had done in the castle's kitchen earlier that day, one would think I should have worked up quite the appetite. Oh, well. I would eat enough to help me recover something of my strength, and no more.

"We were preparing as well," Corin said then as he set down his fork and reached for his goblet. "It is Lord Sorthannic's custom at the harvest ball to bring out some bottles from the harvest of three years earlier, and to share them with his guests. He was there today, consulting with Master Brinsell as to which ones would work best with this year's menu."

So the great man had deigned to visit the cellars? I supposed he must, for this was a matter that directly reflected upon his hospitality. "That must be a somewhat difficult task, given the number of courses Brynna has planned for the feast."

Corin shot me a sideways look at that remark, as though he had detected the bitterness which underlaid my words. However, when he spoke, his tone was mild enough. "His Grace has more than a hundred guests coming. I would assume that such a number would require a veritable mountain of food."

All prepared by the drudges in the kitchen… myself among them. Quarreling over such an obvious fact seemed like a foolish waste of time, though, so I merely nodded and said, "Yes, it is a great deal more than what we are used to, but Brynna has it all well in hand. I am sure it will all go well, and his lordship's guests will have another magnificent feast to talk about until next year's ball comes 'round."

"I do get the impression that Brynna tries to outdo herself each year. Master Brinsell says that those of us working in the cellars will get trays of food brought to us, and so I will have a chance to sample some of that magnificence."

Favored treatment, indeed. True, Lynnis had said that the leftovers would be sent to the settlement for all of us to enjoy, but that was not quite the same thing as being able to partake of such delicacies while they were still fresh and hot. But I supposed that Lord Sorthannic viewed his workers in the cellar as more valuable than the rest of us, since without the contributions of those who helped to make his wines, he would have no reason to even host a harvest ball.

Once again I decided to keep my trenchant observations to myself. "That sounds lovely," I said, my tone neutral. "After my clumsy efforts in the kitchen, I have no doubt that being able to sample Brynna's offerings will be a veritable treat."

My comment caused Corin to raise an eyebrow, then set down his fork. "I do not think they are clumsy," he said. "Perhaps not as elaborate as what Brynna serves at the castle, but I could not expect that of you, for I am only a simple laborer, and not a peer of the realm like Lord Sorthannic."

Once I could have been counted as such, as the daughter of a wealthy baron. I inwardly scolded myself for such a thought, because my father had given me the opportunity to reclaim that part of myself, and I had turned him down. And all for love of the man who sat across the table from me, the man who seemed now more of a stranger than when I had known him barely at all. I could not help but get the sense that he made conversation with me only because it would have been awkward to sit there in silence while we ate.

Because I could not think of how else to respond, I offered him a wan smile and said, "Thank you, Corin. I want to do what I can to make things pleasant for you."

"And you do." He paused then, goblet still in his hand, the flickers of the candle flame picking up warm gleams in the biscuit-colored glaze of the stoneware. "Please never think that I don't know everything you have had to sacrifice to be here with me."

The words were innocent enough...indeed, were warmer than any of his most recent utterances had been. Even so, I could not help but experience a small pang of worry. Had he somehow caught wind of my father's visit here? Of course I had not said anything, and the weather had been so foul that evening, I did not think any of my neighbors had been out and about to witness his arrival. Still, I could not be certain that someone had not seen him come to our little hamlet, especially since the arrival of a man on horseback would have been worthy of note.

Perhaps it would have been better to tell Corin the truth, but I found I could not bring myself to do so. Cowardly, yes, but an impulse that sprang from wishing to avoid a confrontation, rather than because I was attempting to hide something shameful.

"I do not think it any great sacrifice," I murmured, and then popped a bite of chicken pie in my mouth so I would not have to say anything further.

For a long moment, my husband watched me, eyes slightly narrowed. Anything he had intended to say, however, it seemed he decided to keep to himself, for after taking another sip of wine, he set down his goblet and returned to the food on his plate.

And I—I could not allow myself a sigh of relief, but I felt the way my body relaxed as I ate another mouthful of pie. We continued our meal in silence, and I thanked the gods that Corin had granted me that small measure of peace. I would need it, to fortify myself against the hectic day to come.

CHAPTER 14

I SLEPT BETTER THAN I HAD ANY RIGHT TO EXPECT, which was good, for when I arrived at the kitchen the next morning, I was immediately flung into chaos. A veritable mountain of vegetables waited for me to chop them, and Brynna was running to and fro, less a woman than a blur in a brown dress.

But at least I knew what was expected of me and set to at once, glad I had been given a task that, while tedious, was simple enough to manage and not terribly taxing. Poor Alyse was getting quite the scolding, for she had not yet set out the bread to rise, and Nerys also received a tongue-lashing when she nearly upset the pot that held the wild berry sauce for the roast boar, which even now was turning on a spit longer than I was tall.

Somehow, though, we managed to avoid utter catastrophe, and as the day wore on, a bewildering number of dishes began to pile up on the long wooden counters in the kitchen. Tubers in honey sauce, and the roast boar, and a venison ragout, and platters of roasted pheasant and quail, along with a dizzying array of vegetables, either roasted or in sauces rich with herbs and butter. Mountains of bread and rolls, and flavored butters to accompany them, and off to one side, the desserts as well, pies and cakes and custards and creams. Yes, I knew that Lord Sorthannic had more than a hundred guests coming to the feast, and yet it seemed to me that here was food enough to feed five times that number. The banquets my father used to host appeared as simple picnic lunches compared to all this splendor.

Toward the late afternoon, there was a bit of a lull, just enough for me to slip away from the kitchen and hurry toward the entrance of the great hall. At that hour, no guests would yet have arrived, and so I thought it safe enough to peek around the corner and catch a glimpse of the chamber where all the food we had prepared would be consumed.

And oh, my boldness was rewarded, for I saw a great room with tall arched windows of stained glass, and heavy chandeliers of cunningly wrought iron, all swagged with autumn leaves in hues of red and gold and umber. More garlands of brightly colored leaves marched down the centers of the long tables, already set with gleaming pewter plates and expensive glass goblets. Through a tall, arched doorway flanked by pillars of carved rosy marble, I caught just a glimpse of what must be the ballroom, with yet more chandeliers, and more autumn leaves decorating the light fixtures and the tops of the windows. No tables, of course, for that expansive floor must be left open for the dancers.

At that thought, a pang went through me. I did love to dance, and although I had enjoyed the celebration at the settlement to commemorate the crush, taking a few turns on hard-packed earth was not quite the same thing as being able to dance on a polished oak floor, with hundreds of candles flickering overhead to light the way. Why, I could almost imagine the feel of the fine silk gowns I used to wear, the way they would whisper across the wooden floor as my partner turned me under his arm.

Tears stung my eyes, and I blinked them away. It was foolish of me to long for something I would never have again. I reminded myself that I had enjoyed the dancing at the crush very well, for I had been able to hold Corin's hand, to have his arm around my waist. Was that not better than a hundred grand ballrooms, a thousand silken gowns?

"Enough with the peeking," came a crisp voice at my shoulder, and I started, then turned to see Nerys standing before me, hands planted on her broad hips. "Brynna was asking for you— she needs you to wash and hull the berries for the custard."

"I'll be right there," I said, worry and guilt flooding through me. It had been foolish to sneak off like this. I could not afford to anger Brynna so much that she dismissed me. If such a thing were to come to pass, how would Corin and I make it through the winter?

"Yes, you'd better," Nerys replied. Her expression softened somewhat, and she added, "Don't look so stricken, girl. Just get back to work. Brynna is so beside herself, I doubt she has any idea how long you've been gone."

I nodded and went scampering back to the kitchen, where indeed the cook was so preoccupied with adding precise measures of salt to a sauce that she did not even look up when I appeared. As Nerys had said, there was now a large pile of blackberries and raspberries that needed to be cleaned and any bits of stalks and husks removed. I wondered where on earth Brynna had procured the berries, as we were far past their season here in Marric's Rest. Perhaps she had sent for them from some farm far in the south, where the nights had not yet become chilly, and a false summer still lay over the land.

Time wore on, and once I was done with the berries, I was dispatched to help with whipping enough cream to garnish all the desserts we had created. Indeed, I whipped so much cream that it began to feel as though my arm intended to fall right off, but I kept at it doggedly, knowing I dare not stop until Brynna told me I had made enough.

At last, though, she took the bowl away, and I blinked and glanced around the kitchen, realizing that the mountains of food we had prepared had slowly begun to disappear. Indeed, the daylight coming through the clerestory windows high up in the wall had also disappeared, and candles and lanterns had taken their place, and I had not even noticed.

Clearly, the feast was about to begin.

I knew better than to ask if I might go home, however. While the bulk of my work was done, there were always small details that might need my attention. I doubted I would be allowed to leave until the last cake, pie, or custard had been brought into the ballroom—if, of course, Lord Sorthannic followed the usual customs and had his guests adjourn for a set of dancing before they began to consume their dessert.

Brynna had taken some pity on her kitchen staff, and had set aside several platters of roasted chicken, and bowls of rice and potatoes, which Nerys and Alyse were already beginning to dole out onto some plates that had been provided. I was just about to get in line behind them for my own turn when Brynna appeared. Standing behind her was Master Lewyn, Lord Sorthannic's steward. My eyes widened in shock at the sight of such an august personage deigning to visit the kitchen, especially when he must have duties at the feast that should have claimed his attention.

The two of them both wore grim expressions, and my heart sank. Had I done something wrong? As much as I wracked my brains, I could not think of any transgressions I might have committed that would have warranted the presence of Master Lewyn.

All the same, I dropped a quick curtsey, for the steward warranted even more respect than the cook, who usually received a bob of the head and not much more.

"She will do," he said to Brynna, barely looking at me. "See that she is tidied up a bit before you send her out."

"Of course, Master Lewyn," Brynna said, also giving a curtsey, albeit not quite as deep as mine. But perhaps that had more to do with her older knees not being able to manage the task than any lack of respect.

He gave her an offhand nod and went back down the corridor that led to the banquet hall. I sent Brynna a puzzled glance, although a certain suspicion had already begun to grow in me, one that quite made my stomach twist up in knots.

"Take off that apron," Brynna commanded. "Do you have a comb?"

My fingers began to fumble with the strings of the apron at the back of my neck, even as I inquired, "A comb, mistress?"

"Never mind." She hurried away from me, going to the little cubbyhole at the back of the kitchen that she used as a sort of impromptu office. After digging around in a box on the table there, she produced a wooden comb and came back to where I stood. "Tidy your hair as best you can."

I reached up and felt how a few stray strands had escaped from the knot at the back of my neck. Knowing I could not argue, I took the comb from her and smoothed them away from my face, and rearranged the pins that held the heavy braided bun in place. "May I ask why all this primping is necessary?"

Her mouth, bracketed by a series of fine lines, pinched itself even smaller, making her look like one of those dolls that village women sometimes fashioned out of dried apples. "Lysanne has fallen and twisted her ankle. All of the castle's chambermaids have already been assigned to assist the footmen with the feast, and so Master Lewyn came to me and requested the comeliest of my kitchen helpers to take her place." Brynna's mouth tightened even further, as if she did not much like admitting that I was the prettiest of the kitchen servants. Not that it was an accolade I could take too much pride in, for the other women I worked with were not the sort to turn a man's head. "You will go out and help the other maids—the guests are still just arriving, so there is time before the feast begins for you to get your bearings."

Now that the situation I had been dreading had been articulated so clearly, I could feel the terror awake somewhere in my midsection, seeming almost like a wild thing. "Please—is there no one else?"

That question elicited a quite fearsome

frown. Brynna crossed her arms and looked at me as though she had never seen me before. "I have already told you that there is no one else. Really, it is lighter work than what you have been doing in the kitchen all day. You will only need to make sure that the guests' plates and glasses are kept filled to their satisfaction, and after the feast is over, you will help to clear everything away. Do you understand?"

Oh, yes, I understood all too well. I would have to go and mingle with the guests—and possibly catch the eye of Lord Sorthannic himself. So far I had been able to avoid him, buried in the kitchen as I had been, but I could not hope that my luck would hold if I was forced to go out in public, so to speak. I tried to tell myself that I was being overly dramatic, that in a room filled with more than a hundred guests, and probably a score of maidservants and foot-men, it would take a stroke of spectacularly bad luck for the duke to notice me at all.

Besides, I knew I had no choice. If I defied Brynna in this, I would most surely lose my post.

"Yes, I understand," I said meekly.

"Then go, and do as you've been instructed."

I nodded, then turned and went down the same corridor I had traversed a few hours earlier. Then, I had been filled with anticipation, glad of the opportunity to steal a peek at the splendor of the banquet hall, but now cold dread curdled my stomach, making me glad that I had not eaten anything lately. My hands shook, and I knotted them in the heavy linen of my skirt, even as I told myself not to be such a dramatic fool, that no one was going to pay the slightest bit of attention to another maidservant in drab clothing. I supposed I should be glad that I hadn't managed to spill anything on myself during that long day, so at least I appeared somewhat presentable...if anyone would even notice. To my shame, I realized that the servants in the houses where I had visited had often seemed almost invisible to me. They were there only to see to my comfort, and the comfort of the other guests, and I had never paid very much attention to their appearance. I was not proud of such an attitude, and yet I hoped that Lord Sorthannic's guests would behave much the same way, and pay no attention to me. It was the only way I thought I might survive the evening.

When I entered the great hall where the feast was to be held, it seemed that the attendees had not yet come here, that they must still be in his Grace's audience chamber. Lord Sorthannic was nowhere to be seen, which of course made complete sense. He would be with his guests, not here where the last of the platters of food were still being arranged on the long tables set up against the far wall. At an event with this many attendees, it did not make sense to bring out the dishes one by one, as was generally the custom at smaller dinner parties.

"Here," said one of the maidservants, a pretty girl with curly black hair who looked to be a few years younger than I. She handed a platter of tiny stuffed quail to me. "See if you can make room for this on the last table to the right—Alinda has managed to spill some of the wine she was just bringing out, and I must help her with cleaning it up before anyone notices."

"Of course," I replied, then took the tray of quail from her and made haste to the table in question, which fairly groaned with food. How on earth could I ever make room for the platter I held amongst all that extravagance?

But then I spied a small opening between a platter piled high with slices of smoked ham, and a large bowl of what appeared to be jellied rhubarb. If I were very careful, I should be able to slide the platter I held in between the two of them. No doubt if she were present, Brynna would scold me for such a haphazard arrangement, for I was certain there was supposed to be an order in which the dishes were presented on the tables. However, she was busy elsewhere, and I knew I needed to relieve myself of the burden I carried so I would be available to fill plates and wine goblets once the guests began to enter the hall. The quail were identifiable enough; the other servers should be able to locate them without too much difficulty.

Balancing the platter on my left hip, I reached out with my right hand to push the bowl of jellied rhubarb off to one side so I might slide the tray of quail in between the two. All seemed to be going well enough—until I poked at the bowl one last time to move it an inch or so more. Before I could really grasp what was happening, the bowl slipped off the edge of the slick damask tablecloth and crashed to the stone floor. Even worse, the wreck of the rhubarb startled me so much that I also let go of the platter I'd precariously planted on one hip, stuffed quail scattering everywhere.

"Oh, no!" I exclaimed, and at once fell to my knees and began desperately picking up the tiny roasted birds and depositing them on the platter. There was no way I could put them out for the duke's guests to eat, but I also could not leave them where they were. And oh, once Brynna caught wind of my clumsiness, she would surely dismiss me! What would I ever tell Corin? Would he understand that it had been a simple accident, and that I hadn't done such a thing to avoid being around Lord Sorthannic?

"Let me help," said a familiar voice, and I looked up to see a handsome man sumptuously dressed in a velvet doublet and high polished boots staring down at me. A shining silver circlet set with garnets held back his heavy dark hair. Smiling, he went on, "It can be our little secret."

My breath caught and strangled in my throat. Was I going mad? I must be. Otherwise, I could not explain the apparition who stood before me now.

The man in the velvet doublet was my husband Corin.

CHAPTER 15

No, it could not be. It wasn't possible. As I continued to stare at him, dumbfounded, I saw that this man's eyes were not my husband's dark, rich brown, but a cool blue, unusual for a man of Sirlende. In fact, I thought I had only ever met one man whose eyes were that same shade.

Lord Sorthannic Sedassa, Duke of Marric's Rest.

He must have seen my bewilderment and alarm, for he reached out and laid a hand on my wrist, his touch gentle, clearly meant to reassure me. "It is all right, Marenna. I am Corin, your husband...but I am also the lord of this estate."

What kind of sorcery was this? I, who was rarely at a loss for words, could only stare at him, thinking this must be some kind of mad dream born of my worry about my marriage, my anxiety that I would somehow do something to embarrass myself while assisting with the preparations for the duke's feast.

And yet the sensation of his strong fingers against my flesh was real enough. More than real —familiar, every callus, every brush of his work-roughened skin. Work-roughened? Such a detail must be a product of my imagination, for how could a duke have anything but soft hands that had never seen a day's labor?

Those eyes, though—the color might be wrong, but in shape they were my husband's, as were the heavy dark lashes, the straight dark brows. I searched my memories to recall what I could remember of Lord Sorthannic's appearance the one and only time I had seen him, but truly, his face had been so covered by that bird's nest of a beard, and his hair so long and wild, that I could not remember any details with any clarity. Only the color of his eyes, so unusual. The same eyes that stared at me now, pleading for me to understand.

It was too much. Something inside me seemed to break, and I made a panicked little sound, then pushed myself to my feet and fled the chamber and the mess I had made, ran from him. I did not want to acknowledge the possibility that his words might be true, for then I would have to also admit that my entire life with Corin had been a lie.

He caught up with me easily enough, for his legs were much longer than mine. Within the minute, I was trapped in the corridor that connected the kitchen and banquet hall—a corridor that should have been filled with servants rushing to bring the last few dishes to the serving table, or possibly beginning to take the desserts to the ballroom, if the main courses had all been put in place. However, now that same corridor was conspicuously empty, which made me think that Corin—Lord Sorthannic— must have given the order for everyone to stay away.

Oh, he looked very grand and terrible looming over me as he did now, so much taller in his fine black velvet doublet and high gleaming black boots and the heavy jeweled chain draped over his broad shoulders than he'd appeared in the simple clothes he had worn while pretending to be Corin, a laborer with no true home. I shrank into an alcove that was some- times used to store serving carts, and wished myself a thousand miles away. Unfortunately, I possessed no magic, and so remained exactly where I was.

However, I was not so over-awed that I would allow him to speak first. "You lied to me!"

The accusation seemed to draw him up short. He crossed his arms and stared down at me, his expression one of thwarted anger. "Perhaps I misrepresented."

"Which is the same thing as a lie," I retorted. "How could you lead me to believe that you were only Corin Blackstone, when in fact you are the lord of this estate?"

"Because your pride and your arrogance—and yes, your unruly tongue—led me to think that you needed to learn a lesson in humility, and acceptance. I wanted you for my wife, Marenna, but I also needed to know that you wanted me for myself, not merely as the lord of these lands, someone who could give you a title even greater than the one to which you were born, along with a life of more luxury than even you were used to."

"Oh, indeed?" Ignoring the pleading expression in his eyes, I went on, "And so your own fragile pride could not allow a wife who was impressed by your title, your wealth? Who is the arrogant one here, your Grace?"

"Sorthannic," he corrected me at once, and then grimaced. "Thani, actually. I have a distinct loathing of my given name, no matter that it is a traditional one for the men in the Sedassa family."

Even as angry as I was right then, I had to admit that "Thani" suited him much better. "Very well, *Thani*. Clearly, everyone on your estate must have known the truth. Have they all been laughing at me, smiling at my foolishness behind my back?"

"Not at all," he said. His hand slid down from my wrist so he might entwine his fingers with mine. As much as I wanted to pull my hand from his grasp, I did not quite dare. And also...also, I did rather like the sensation of his skin brushing against mine. "Indeed, Master Brinsell made his disapproval of the scheme quite known. But I assured him you would come to no harm, and so he relented."

No harm? I wondered if Thani would have allowed the charade to continue until my shoes were utterly ruined, and I was forced to walk to work in the kitchen in my bare feet. In that moment, I recalled how I had asked my father to bring me some of the shoes I had left behind.

My father....

Bright realization flared, and I snatched my fingers from Thani's. His brows drew together, but I noted how he did not attempt to retain his grip on my hand. "You plotted this with my father, didn't you?"

"Yes," he replied, his tone even. To his credit, he did not look away, but held my gaze. Those eyes of his were so very blue, like a cabochon sapphire ring my mother had bequeathed to me, and which I had hated to leave behind at Silverhold.

A woman could drown in those eyes, I thought.

Thani continued, "I will admit that I went to your father and told him I wanted nothing more than to marry you, but that I thought you spoiled and in need of some humbling."

"'Spoiled'?" I repeated, not sure I had heard him right. How in the world could Thani have thought me spoiled? "When I have made your meals for you every day, kept the cottage clean, worked in this very castle's kitchens?"

"You have shown yourself to be brave and strong, my love. No, you are not spoiled...now. But I think it is fair enough to say that you are not precisely the same woman you were when you left your father's house a ten-day ago."

How could I argue with such a statement when I had thought much the same thing myself? This time away from the shelter of my father's house had taught me much about self-reliance, about throwing away my "shoulds" and "oughts" and focusing on what needed to be done. Still, my heart ached with what I could only see as betrayal on my father's part. How could he have done such a thing to me?

Perhaps sensing my inner turmoil, Thani once again reached out to me, both hands taking mine. I could have pulled away...but found I did not much wish to. Voice low, but warm and worried at the same time, he said, "Did you really think your father so heartless as to send you away with a complete stranger? He knows you well enough that he could tell you felt some attraction to me, despite your harsh words. When I went to speak with him afterward and tell him of my plan, he only agreed to it because he knew that I would make sure you were always kept safe. And also—"

"Also what?" I cut in, wondering what other humiliating revelations I would be forced to suffer.

"Also, I vowed to him that I would not make you my wife in reality until you knew the truth about me. I did not want to make love to you as Corin Blackstone, Marenna...I wanted to do so only as Sorthannic Sedassa...your true husband."

The ache in his voice as he uttered those words was almost palpable. Now I understood the forced coldness, the way he had turned away from me just as I finally unbent enough to reach out to him. He wanted me but had made a promise to my father, which meant this husband of mine was a man of his word, no matter how much it might cost him.

"And so when my father came to visit me the other day...."

"Forgive me for that." Thani lifted my hands to his lips, kissed first one palm, and then the other. Delicious shivers rippled all through my body, and I knew I would not shrink away from him, not when he had such an intoxicating effect on me. "It was one last test. I needed to know for sure that you truly did love me for myself. I thought if you did not care, then you would eagerly go away with your father, would hurry to reclaim your title and the life of ease you'd been forced to leave behind you. But you told him no, that you would choose no other life than the one you had now. Once I heard that, I knew I could trust you completely."

I wanted to retort that I had given him ample reason for trust, even before that day. But then I recalled how his heart had been broken by the Crown Princess, how he had been so sure of her love, only to have it rejected so she might travel to Keshiaar and marry the ruler of that far-off land. What a blow that must have been, even if Thani had done his best to convince himself that Princess Lyarris had done so only to fulfill her duties as the Emperor's sister. No wonder he had needed to be certain of me. A heart thus wounded would find it difficult to trust in another.

"Yes, you can trust me, Thani," I said. "I will not lie to you and say I am not still angry about this subterfuge, but I think I can understand the reasons behind it. But I would be your wife in a cottage, and I will be your wife in this castle—if you will have me."

"Oh, yes, I will have you." A wicked light gleamed in his blue eyes, reminding me of another question I needed to have answered.

I tilted my head up at him. "If there are to be no secrets between us, then tell me how it is your eyes are blue, but Corin Blackstone's were so very dark brown?"

He grinned and reached into the pouch of tooled leather that hung from his belt. From within he pulled out the heavy silver ring with the twistwork design he had worn all his days as "Corin." "This little bauble," he told me. "A minor enchantment, one performed by my sister, who was experimenting to see whether she could cast spells on objects rather than people, and have the effects of those spells last indefinitely. A very small alteration when I wear it, making my blue eyes brown. I thought that was all the situation required, since I looked so very different already once I shaved off my beard and trimmed my hair."

As I watched, he slipped the ring on his finger. At once his eyes darkened, and there was Corin Blackstone gazing down on me. Just as swiftly, his appearance changed again as he pulled the ring from his hand and put it back in the pouch.

"No wonder magic is forbidden," I said, my tone somewhat shaky, "if you can perform such wonders with it."

"Oh, this is nothing. As I said, a minor enchantment. And I rather think the Emperor is doing his best to change some of those laws. The days when the world could be broken in two by the spells of the warrior-mages is long gone, and all that are left are small magics such as these." Thani shrugged. "But that is no concern of mine. My sister dwells in a land where magic is not outlawed, and so may do as she pleases. And we—well, we are missing our own wedding feast."

"Our what?" I asked. For yes, I knew that Thani was absent from the very gala he was supposed to be hosting, but this was no wedding feast and dance, only his traditional harvest ball.

"It seemed the right occasion to introduce you to the world," he said. "Do you think my encountering you just as you spilled those plates was an accident? I needed to speak with you in private, to end this game I was playing. I want everyone to see you as my wife, Marenna."

"I am so very sorry about that—" I began, and he smiled and shook his head.

"Do not worry. The mess has already been cleaned up, and the maids who undertook the task will find a nice reward of a silver piece each awaiting them for their trouble."

Yet more evidence of his generous heart. There were not so many lords who would have thought to compensate their maids for doing such a thing, for most would have considered it simply part of their duties and not deserving of any additional notice. But still....

"I—" As much as I wanted this charade to end as well, I could not help but look down at myself in dismay, at the plain clothing I wore, at the wrinkles in my skirt—and several new stains, courtesy of dropping that platter of roasted quail and having stuffing and grease spatter my clothes. "You cannot think that I would go in front of all your guests looking like this?"

"Of course not," Thani replied with a smile. "Come, my love—let us begin your transformation into the Duchess of Marric's Rest."

ॐ

He led me upstairs by means of a hidden staircase, up several flights of steps and down a long corridor, until we came to a large set of carved doors. Behind those doors was a suite of such sumptuousness that it quite put my own rooms at Silverhold to shame—columns of carved wood, hangings of silk and velvet, every inch of the stone floors covered in priceless Keshiaari rugs. A cheerful applewood fire burned in a hearth of warm-hued marble.

And there was Sendra, coming forth from one of the rooms beyond the sitting chamber where Thani and I entered the suite. She was smiling, but I also saw how tears glistened in her eyes when she looked upon me. Was it that I appeared now so drab and plain, so changed from the Marenna she remembered? I was not sure I wanted to know.

"Here is your charge," Thani said, also smiling. "I know you will work your magic—but do not take too long, for our guests are waiting, and

I am sure my wife is hungry after her labors today."

"No more than twenty minutes," Sendra promised, and I could not quite prevent myself from raising an eyebrow. Back at my father's house, preparations for one of our own balls could take as much as three hours.

It seemed that Thani affected not to notice my skepticism, for he nodded and said, "Bring her down when she is ready." He bent and kissed me on the cheek. "I will see you in a short while, my love. But now I must go, lest everyone think I have been spirited away from my own party."

What could I do except murmur my agreement, and watch him exit the chamber? Almost as soon as he was gone, Sendra came up to me and said, "Oh, it is so good to see you, my lady. We do not have time to wash and dry your hair, but I have a bath waiting, and once you are done with that, I will get you dressed."

A real bath, one that had not required me to heat ewer after ewer of water over the fire? It sounded heavenly.

I followed her into the bath chamber, and there was a tub of marble, filled with water smelling of lavender. There was so much I wanted to ask—had she also known of the plot my father and Thani had hatched between them?—but I knew we did not have time for such things. I could not even enjoy the bath as much as I would have liked, for after a scant few minutes I had to climb back out again, and have Sendra hand me a silk chemise and silk underdrawers and stockings. I dressed myself in those underthings, then sat down so she might brush out my hair and arrange it in a mass of complicated coils and braids…but no curls, for we did not have time for such niceties.

Not that I minded so much when I saw the dress that had been laid out for me, silk damask in a rich wine color, trimmed in gold and embroidered in pearls. "Where on earth did this come from?" I asked as Sendra laced me into the garment.

"Oh, his Grace ordered it for you. 'Twas no great task to have it made up, since I used one of the dresses you left behind at Silverhold as the pattern."

That made sense. There would have been plenty of time to construct such a gown during the days I had lived in my cottage with Corin—Thani, that is. And there were slippers of gilded leather sewn with gold thread and more pearls, and combs of gold and garnet and pearls to be tucked into my hair. Then at last a heavy necklace with large garnet pendants bordered in seed pearls, and earrings and a ring and bracelets to match. Even I, who had left behind a fairly impressive collection of jewelry, felt my eyes widen as I looked on the pieces Thani had given me to wear.

And when we were done, and Sendra brought me to look on the result of her handiwork in the large walnut-framed mirror that hung on one wall—why, I could barely recognize myself. True, it had been nearly two weeks since I had last seen my own reflection, and yet I thought this alteration was something more than that. The Marenna who gazed back at me seemed a different woman, more serious, a certain soberness in her dark eyes that had not been there a fortnight ago. This woman looked as though she could be a duchess.

"Oh, you are the most beautiful woman in the kingdom," Sendra said, her hands clasped together as she gazed upon me.

"I am not so sure about that, but as long his Grace is pleased by my appearance, then all is well."

"Oh, he will be most pleased. But you must go now, my lady—I will show you the way."

I began to thank her, but a more pressing notion popped into my mind. "Sendra, you will be staying here with us, won't you?"

A flush touched her cheeks. "I would like that very much, my lady. If it is what you wish."

"Oh, it is," I assured her. Somehow learning how to be a duchess did not sound quite so frightening if I could negotiate those pathways with my faithful lady's maid at my side.

She dropped a curtsey. "Then of course I will be here for you."

I reached out and squeezed her hand, then quickly let go, for it was time for her to lead me from the suite and down another staircase—not the narrow one Thani had used to bring me here, one which I guessed was intended for the servants' use, but a grand affair of marble with carved walnut banisters on either side—and on into the banquet hall, which was crowded with more than a hundred beautifully dressed people, all of whose eyes were immediately fixed upon me.

Hot blood rushed to my cheeks, and I had to fight the urge to flee. But there was Thani, coming to me so he might take me by the hand and proudly announce, "Noble lords and ladies —I give you Marenna Sedassa, Duchess of Marric's Rest!"

Everyone broke into applause, which only made my cheeks flush that much more. But I did not have time to be too embarrassed, for Thani led me to the high table, where my father and my brothers and their wives waited, all dressed in their finest. Having those familiar faces around me, all of them so clearly happy to see me so settled, made me feel somewhat more at ease. And there, too, were Hal and Lynnis, both of them finely dressed, he in a handsome wool doublet in a rich wine color, and she in a green silk damask gown that brought out the color of her beautiful eyes.

To my surprise, she was seated on my right, and shot me a wicked smile as I stared at her in surprise. It had been so good of Thani to include my friends in the banquet, but I hadn't thought they would be able to sit with us at the high table.

"Your husband is not much of one for pomp and circumstance," she murmured in my ear as the same pretty black-eyed maidservant who had spoken to me earlier came up to the table and began to pour wine for all of us. "To him, we are your friends, and our station matters very little. I suppose that is what comes from having a 'commoner' for a mother."

I flushed at the word, for I recalled all too well how I had spoken it to Lynnis not so long ago when discussing the duke—my husband, that is. But I thought that she probably had the truth of the matter, for Thani had not spent his entire life in Sirlende, being waited on hand and foot, but had come here as a youth after knowing what it was like to work in his family's fields, to know the happiness of a day spent in doing something one loved.

"Well, I am very glad to hear it," I replied. "For while I do not think I will miss scrubbing the floors, I would have missed you and Hal very much, if my new rank were to forever separate us."

"No need to worry on that front. Indeed, his Grace is already talking about having a new house built for us in the spring, now that we are expecting this little one." Her hand touched her gown at her waist, although of course she was not showing at all yet. "I suppose it is a way of showing respect for the new under-overseer."

"Oh, is Hal to be given that position?" I asked, happier than ever for the two of them.

"Yes, because it is true enough about Master Threnson. He has no desire to take up his work again after his leg has healed, and your husband has said he will give him enough money to get settled in the city, hopefully in an occupation that is more to his taste."

Again I could not help but be impressed by Thani's generosity. When faced with such goodness, I found that I could not hold on to what little of my anger remained. Yes, he and my father—and, it seemed, almost everyone here on the estate—had been involved in the plan to hide the truth of "Corin's" identity, but no harm had come to me.

Indeed, in that moment I believed that I would have been very much worse off, if it were not for the way Thani had shown me a way to live a better life.

The feast was a merry one, although I knew I could not sample even a third of all the dishes I had helped to prepare. And again, each of them had more savor, because I knew of all the effort which had gone into them, all the care and thought.

At last, though, the feast was over, and all of us guests moved into the ballroom so the servants might begin to clear away the empty dishes and glasses and platters from the banquet hall. The musicians on the dais at the far end of the room immediately struck the first chord for the *verdralle,* and it was time for all those inclined to dance to find their partners, and begin the sweeping movements of the dance.

And oh, how wonderful to have Thani take me in his arms and hold me close as we began to make our circuit of the dance floor, my senses nearly overwhelmed by the gleam of the candles and the warm hues of the swags of autumn leaves that decorated the chandeliers and the windows. His clothing smelled of cloves, warm and spicy, as delicious as he was.

As we swirled around, I caught glimpses of those who had decided to stand and watch rather than dance. There was my father, beaming as he looked upon Thani and me, and there, too, were my brothers and their wives, wearing their best smiles, and Hal and Lynnis, who perhaps had decided to wait out this one because of her delicate condition. Yes, my family had not been there to witness my marriage to the Duke of Marric's Rest, but at least he had made sure to give me a wedding feast and ball that would be the envy of any woman.

"Happy?" he asked, and I nodded.

"Almost too happy."

His blue eyes glinted down at me. "Can one be too happy?"

I pretended to consider. "I am not entirely sure. I suppose that is something we will have to put to the test."

"Challenge accepted, your Grace."

And even though we danced in front of everyone, he bent and kissed me fully on the mouth. Not too deep or too lingering a kiss, but a

promise of things yet to come. I had thought I
could not feel more alive than I did already,
swirling about the dance floor while held firmly
in his arms, but the touch of his lips on mine
awoke a fever within me, one that I knew would
finally be slaked.

First, though, we had to make our way
through the rest of the evening, which passed in
something of a joyful blur. I spoke with my
father, assuring him that I had already forgiven
him for the subterfuge he and Thani had perpe-
trated, and I accepted the congratulations of my
brothers and sisters-in-law, and many others who
were only names to me, but who I hoped would
become my friends in the future.

At last, though, Thani and I were able to bid
farewell to our guests, and climb the stairs to
our suite. Within, all was in readiness, a fire
dancing in the hearth, the embroidered coverlet
on the bed already turned down, a decanter of
wine and two glasses waiting on a table in the
sitting area. He poured wine for the two of us,
and we drank to our health and our shared
future.

But then he set down his glass, his expression
quite serious. From a pocket in his doublet, he
drew out a heavy gold ring set with diamonds,
then slipped it onto my finger. I had to blink back

tears, for I had felt the lack of a wedding ring keenly. Now I truly felt that we were married.

Voice soft but urgent, he asked, "Will you be my wife, Marenna?"

I knew precisely what he asked of me. In the eyes of the gods and of the world, we were already man and wife. However, the two of us knew better. We must be together now, in the manner Lynnis had spoken of.

The shiver that went through me then was not one of fear, but of delicious anticipation. "Oh, yes, Thani. Make me your wife."

He came to me, and kissed me, and plucked the combs and pins from my hair so it fell onto my shoulders in a heavy mass, and pulled the drawstring at the neck of my chemise so it was loosened, and I was revealed to him. No time to be embarrassed, for he was caressing me then, touching me in a way that seemed to bring forth a sweet, needy fire within my veins. We fell onto the bed together, arms wrapped around one another, desiring nothing more than a joining that had been delayed for far too long.

And when it was over and I lay in his arms, I could only think of how splendid this was, how splendid *he* was. Thani...Corin...it mattered not. What mattered was the heart and the strength of the man who held me now, who would be my husband in this world and the next.

"What do you think?" he inquired, as he reached up with his free hand to rub his chin while we rested there, supported by soft feather pillows. "Should I grow the beard back?"

"Don't you dare," I replied in mock-severe tones. "Your face is far too handsome to cover up in such a fashion."

"I will not comment on my handsomeness, but I have found that shaving each morning does require an inordinate amount of time."

I rolled over on my side so I might gaze at him, at the fine outline of his profile silhouetted against the fire in the hearth. "If you stop shaving, and return to the state in which I first saw you, then I will have no choice but to call you 'Thrushbeard' all the rest of your life."

"The gods forbid!" He chuckled and pulled me close so he might kiss me again. This late in the evening, his chin had begun to show some scruff, just enough to be pleasantly scratchy against my cheek. "I certainly do not want my wife referring to me as 'Thrushbeard.' So as long as you don't mind the time it takes, then I will do my best to maintain my current appearance."

"I won't mind," I said. "It will make me happy, I think."

A certain glint entered his eyes. "You know that I live to make you happy, Marenna."

"You do?" I asked, my voice somewhat arch. "Perhaps you should prove that to me."

"With pleasure," he said, and pulled me to him again. Another kiss, and another, and then his hands were upon me, his body against mine.

And yes, he had only been telling the simple truth.

He did know exactly how to make me happy.

The End

Dear Readers:

This is the last of the Latter Kingdoms novels—I had originally planned to have *Moon Dance* be the last book in the series. However, fate intervened (as it often does) when I agreed to write a fairy tale–based short story for a fantasy anthology. I chose the tale of King Thrushbeard, as it's a more obscure story and not one that as many people are familiar with, unlike Beauty and the Beast, Cinderella, Rumplestiltskin, or some of the other fairy tales I've retold in this series. Unfortunately, the person organizing the anthology didn't have a formal sign-up sheet or anything like that where we could call "dibs" on the stories we'd chosen, and someone else picked

Thrushbeard as well. Since she'd already written her story, whereas all I'd done was take notes, I begged off and did not participate in the anthology.

But I couldn't quite let go of the story. Since I'd already laid the groundwork—part of which was providing a happy ending for Sorthannic Sedassa, who'd gotten a raw deal in *One Thousand Nights* when Lyarris decided to leave Sirlende and marry the Hierarch of Keshiaar—I decided to go ahead and turn my story idea into a novel. To be honest, that worked out better for me anyway, since I've always had a difficult time writing shorter pieces!

The hard part about retelling fairy tales—for me, anyway—is attempting to give logical motivations for the sometimes capricious decisions of the characters in these very old stories. While the spoiled princess in the original Thrushbeard tale does deserve to get some kind of comeuppance, she's still treated fairly harshly for her transgressions. I tried to soften some of her punishments in this retelling, since the last thing I wanted was for the hero to come off as unsympathetic, although of course he has his own reasons for the trick he plays on the heroine.

And while it's hard to say goodbye to a series, nine is a good number, and that is where I'll leave this one. I've loved every moment I've spent in the world of the Latter Kingdoms, but it's time to move on to new stories, new worlds.

I hope you'll explore those worlds with me!

Christine Pope
Santa Fe, New Mexico
October 2017

ALSO BY CHRISTINE POPE

THE WATCHERS TRILOGY

(Paranormal Romance)

Falling Dark

Dead of Night

Rising Dawn

᳖

THE WITCHES OF CLEOPATRA HILL

(Paranormal Romance)

Darkangel

Darknight

Darkmoon

Sympathetic Magic

Protector

Spellbound

A Cleopatra Hill Christmas

Impractical Magic

Strange Magic

The Arrangement

Defender

Bad Blood

Deep Magic

Darktide

THE DJINN WARS

(Paranormal Romance)

Chosen

Taken

Fallen

Broken

Forsaken

Forbidden

Awoken

Illuminated

THE SEDONA FILES

(Paranormal Romance)

Bad Vibrations

Desert Hearts

Angel Fire

Star Crossed

Falling Angels

Enemy Mine

❧

TALES OF THE LATTER KINGDOMS

(Fantasy Romance)

All Fall Down

Dragon Rose

Binding Spell

Ashes of Roses

One Thousand Nights

Threads of Gold

The Wolf of Harrow Hall

Moon Dance

The Song of the Thrush

❧

THE GAIAN CONSORTIUM SERIES

(Science Fiction Romance)

Blood Will Tell

Breath of Life

The Gaia Gambit

The Mandala Maneuver

The Titan Trap

The Zhore Deception

ABOUT THE AUTHOR

Christine Pope has been writing stories ever since she commandeered her family's Smith-Corona typewriter back in the sixth grade. Her work includes paranormal romance, fantasy romance, and science fiction/space opera romance. She fell under the Land of Enchantment's spell while researching her Djinn Wars series and now makes her home in Santa Fe, New Mexico.

To be notified about new releases by Christine Pope, please go to www.christinepope.com and sign up for her newsletter.